NURSERY FRIENDS from FRANCE

CAMBRAI

YVETOT

BAYEUX

ROUEN

CAEN

PARIS

VERDUN

RENNES

VERSAILLES

NANTES

AUVERGNE

SAVOY

AVIGNON

Nursery Friends from France

Translated by
Olive Beaupré Miller
Illustrated by
Maud and Miska Petersham

Published by
The Book House for Children
Chicago

26

Printed in U. S. A.

FOREWORD

THESE little *chansons*, which take the place of nursery rhymes in France, have been beloved by generations of French children, for most of them are at least a hundred years old. They come to America, bearing the lively, varied rhythms, now gay and bounding in merriment, now sweet and tender, which can well up from no single writer, but only from the hearts of a whole people. There is more of the real France in these rhymes than in volumes of more learned books. And what a kaleidoscope of French life — shepherds and shepherdesses, now from the dainty fancy of a Watteau, now from the rugged reality of a Jules Breton, peasants and princes, citizens and villagers, ploughmen and sailors, lawyers and millers, carpenters and blacksmiths, duchesses and beggars! Now one wanders in shops and city squares, where dames of Paris sweep all day; in a moment, *presto!* there is the countryside — flowery meadows, green fields, and forests, chateaux, thatched cottages and Gothic church spires. This is France and this is the French *chanson*.

May the rhythm of these poems find an echo in the hearts of the children of America!

To Peter and John

If a little boy were to sail away,
　　Yeo ho for the sailor boy!
He'd certainly come to France some day,
　　Yeo ho for the sailor boy!

And there would be meadows, with daisies pied,
Where poppies red and blue corn-flowers hide,
And queer little cottages thatched with straw,
Such hedgerows and church-spires as never you saw!
But ah! no Peter or John would be there;
Nay, only a Jean, or perhaps a Pierre;
And they'd say "Bon jour!" or they'd say, "Parlez vous?"
But never "Good day!" or "How do you do?"

　　Yet the sailor boy would not feel alone,
　　　　Yeo ho for the sailor boy!
　　For in France he'd find some good friends of his own,
　　　　Yeo ho for the sailor boy!

*Nursery Friends
from France*

There's dear Dumollay, always saying Good-by!
And sweet Dame Tartine with her horses of pie!
There's lovely Rosina, the face-making belle,
And that very good fellow, Cadet Rouselle.
There's great la Palisse, as brave as bold,
There's Harlequin, too, and Punch, I'm told.
There's sad Dame Michelle, ever seeking her cat,
And fair Coqueliquette, so big and so fat.

    Ah, the sailor boy would not feel alone,
        Yeo ho for the sailor boy!
    For in France he'd find some good friends of his own,
        Yeo ho for the sailor boy!

There's Duchess Anne in her wooden shoes,
And the bold, brave boy who fled from cuckoos!
There's Yvetot's King, quite simple and gay,
And he with the daughters so fair, Giroflay.
Oh, there is Pierrot by the light of the moon,
And the King of Sardinia, fleeing too soon.
King Dagobert's there with his breeches on wrong,
And other important heroes of song.

    Ah, the sailor boy would not feel alone,
        Yeo ho for the sailor boy!
    For in France he'd find some good friends of his own,
        Yeo ho for the sailor boy!

Nursery Friends
from France

O Father Dear!

O father dear,—
Do ships at sea
Have legs way down below?

Of course they do,
Little goosie, you!
For how else could they go?

Guilleri

There was a little fellow,
His name was Guilleree,—
Carabee!
One day he went a-hunting,
For partridge hunted he,—
Carabee!
Tee-tee, carabee,
To-to, carabo!
Good fellow, Guilleree,
You do intend, you do intend, to risk your life, I see!

To watch his dogs a-running,
He climbed up in a tree,—
Carabee!
The branch began a-cracking,
And down fell Guilleree,—
Carabee!
Tee-tee, carabee,
To-to, carabo!
Good fellow, Guilleree,
You do intend, you do intend, to risk your life, I see!

We Were Ten Maidens

We were ten maidens on the green,
Ready for to wed, I ween!
　　There was Jean,
　　There was Queen,
There were Claudine and Martine;
　　　Ah! Ah!
Cathri-nette and Cathri-nah!
There was pretty, gay Suzon,
And the Duchess Montbazon;
There, also, was Madelaine,
And there was lovely Miss Dumaine!

The King's son came a-passing then,
Made a bow to all the ten;
　　Bowed to Jean,
　　Bowed to Queen,
Bowed to Claudine and Martine;
　　　Ah! Ah!
Cathri-nette and Cathri-nah!
Bowed to pretty, gay Suzon,
And the Duchess Montbazon,
Also bowed to Madelaine;
But ah! he kissed sweet Miss Dumaine.

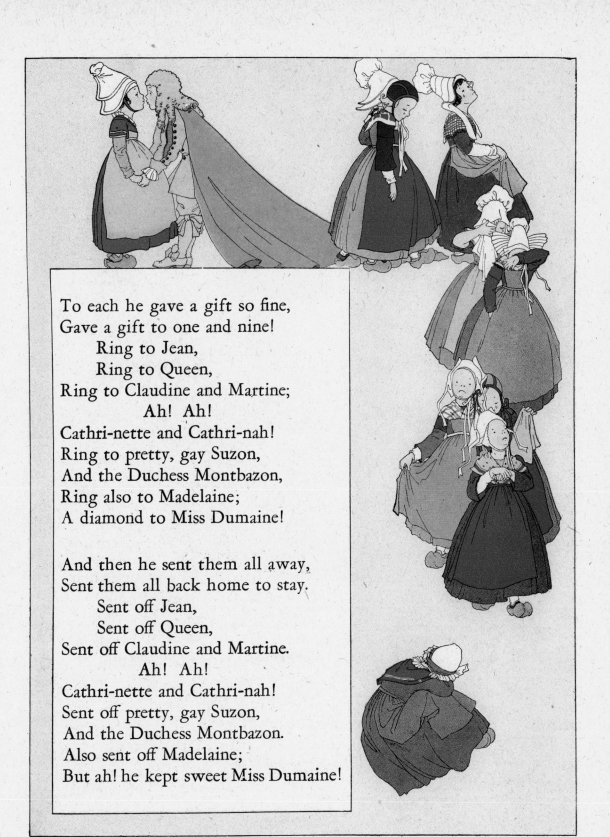

To each he gave a gift so fine,
Gave a gift to one and nine!
　　　Ring to Jean,
　　　Ring to Queen,
Ring to Claudine and Martine;
　　　　Ah! Ah!
Cathri-nette and Cathri-nah!
Ring to pretty, gay Suzon,
And the Duchess Montbazon,
Ring also to Madelaine;
A diamond to Miss Dumaine!

And then he sent them all away,
Sent them all back home to stay.
　　　Sent off Jean,
　　　Sent off Queen,
Sent off Claudine and Martine.
　　　　Ah! Ah!
Cathri-nette and Cathri-nah!
Sent off pretty, gay Suzon,
And the Duchess Montbazon.
Also sent off Madelaine;
But ah! he kept sweet Miss Dumaine!

King Dagobert

King Dagobert once wore
His breeches turned hindside before.
    Said Eloi, the friar:
    "Oh, my King and Sire,
    Those fine clothes on you
    Are all wrong side to!"
The King said: "You don't say?
Then I'll turn them the other way!"

*The chair in this picture was copied from
the golden throne of King Dagobert which
is kept in the treasure chamber of the abbey
at Saint Denis, near Paris, where many of
the kings and queens of France are buried.*

King Dagobert, the brave,
In winter-time never would shave.
　　Said Eloi, the friar:
　　"Oh, my King and Sire,
　　For your chin I hope
　　You'll soon buy some soap!"
The King replied: "Aye! Aye!
Just lend me two sous and I'll buy!"

King Dagobert, so bold,
Went forth as a hunter, I'm told.
　　Said Eloi, the friar:
　　"Oh, my King and Sire,
　　Your poor cheeks are white
　　And you're breathless quite!"
The King replied: "But see,
That rabbit's a-chasing of me!"

Nursery Friends
from France

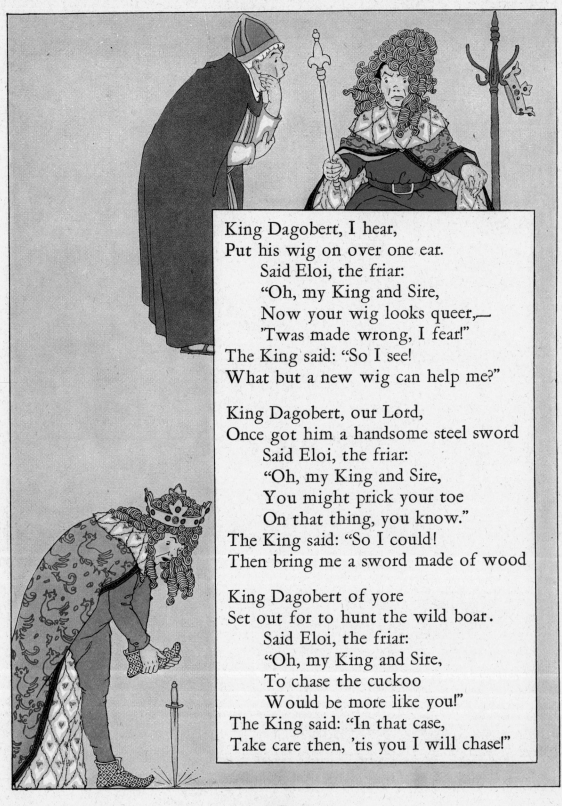

King Dagobert, I hear,
Put his wig on over one ear.
　　Said Eloi, the friar:
　　"Oh, my King and Sire,
　　Now your wig looks queer,—
　　'Twas made wrong, I fear!"
The King said: "So I see!
What but a new wig can help me?"

King Dagobert, our Lord,
Once got him a handsome steel sword
　　Said Eloi, the friar:
　　"Oh, my King and Sire,
　　You might prick your toe
　　On that thing, you know."
The King said: "So I could!
Then bring me a sword made of wood

King Dagobert of yore
Set out for to hunt the wild boar.
　　Said Eloi, the friar:
　　"Oh, my King and Sire,
　　To chase the cuckoo
　　Would be more like you!"
The King said: "In that case,
Take care then, 'tis you I will chase!"

King Dagobert, ah me!
Once thought he'd adventure to sea.
    Said Eloi, the friar:
    "Oh, my King and Sire,
    You might tumble in
    Way up to your chin!"
The King replied: "To think
Men might say I'd gone there to drink!"

King Dagobert was seen
A-wearing his best coat of green.
    Said Eloi, the friar:
    "Oh, my King and Sire,
    You have, I believe,
    A hole in your sleeve!"
The King said: "Can it be?
Your coat's good, so lend it to me!"

King Dagobert at times
Made up the most halting of rhymes.
    Said Eloi, the friar:
    "Oh, my King and Sire,
    'Tis but geese, you know,
    Who make songs, ho! ho!"
The King replied: "I see;
'Tis you then shall make them for me!"

Nursery Friends from France

King Dagobert set forth
One cold day to conquer the earth.
Said Eloi, the friar:
"Oh, my King and Sire,
Now, alas! what if
You should freeze quite stiff!"
The King replied: "Ah, true!
I'd better stay home here with you!"

King Dagobert, the hero of this ridiculous rhyme, was in reality a great and good King of France. He came to the throne in 628 A. D. and was the last worthy descendant of Clovis, before his line, the Merovingians, fell under the iron rule of their Mayors of the Palace. It was King Dagobert's custom to journey throughout his kingdom on horseback, stopping everywhere in towns and villages to hear the complaints of the people and to render justice. So kindly, just and beloved was he, that for generations he was called the great King Dagobert. This song, one of the best-known in France, arose a thousand years or more after his time, a fact which accounts for the ridiculous combination of seventeenth century wigs and breeches with the robes of the seventh century.

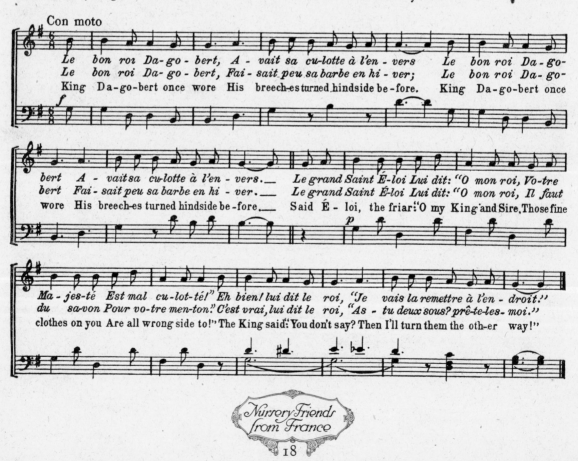

Le bon roi Da-go-bert, A-vait sa cu-lotte à l'en-vers. Le bon roi Da-go-
Le bon roi Da-go-bert, Fai-sait peu sa barbe en hi-ver; Le bon roi Da-go-
King Da-go-bert once wore His breech-es turned hindside be-fore. King Da-go-bert once

bert A-vait sa cu-lotte à l'en-vers.— Le grand Saint É-loi Lui dit: "O mon roi, Vo-tre
bert Fai-sait peu sa barbe en hi-ver.— Le grand Saint É-loi Lui dit: "O mon roi, Il faut
wore His breech-es turned hindside be-fore.— Said É-loi, the friar: "O my King and Sire, Those fine

Ma-jes-té Est mal cu-lot-té!" Eh bien! lui dit le roi, "Je vais la remettre à l'en-droit."
du sa-von Pour vo-tre men-ton?" C'est vrai, lui dit le roi, "As-tu deux sous? prê-te-les-moi."
clothes on you Are all wrong side to!" The King said: "You don't say? Then I'll turn them the oth-er way!"

When Afield Three Hens Do Go

When afield three hens do go,
  First one walks ahead, O ho!
Second follows next, you know!
  Third one walks behind, quite so!
When afield three hens do go,
  First one walks ahead, O ho!

Pingo, Pango,
Nuts are Good!

Way back home there is a wood,
Pingo, pango, nuts are good;—
Where once two little rabbits stood—
Bee-be-lin, Bee-be-lo,
Po-po,
La gay-na-go,
Ho, nuts are good!

I went to hunt them in the wood,
Pingo, pango, nuts are good;—
They hopped off fast as rabbits could!
Bee-be-lin, Bee-be-lo,
Po-po,
La gay-na-go,
Ho, nuts are good!

Don't hunt rabbits in the wood,
Pingo, pango, nuts are good;—
Two at once,—you never should!
Bee-be-lin, Bee-be-lo,
Po-po,
La gay-na-go,
Ho, nuts are good!

So Many Children to Wed Have We

So many children to wed have we,
Our attic's full of them, you see!
Ah, great heavens, now tell me, pray,
How to marry all these away!

Dame Tartine

There was once a dame called Tartine,
Had a butter palace, 'tis said.
Oh, its walls were all of white flour,
And its floors were crisp gingerbread.
    Unless I mistake,
    Her bed-room was cake!
    She slept every night
    On a biscuit light!

When she sallied forth to the town,
She'd a bonnet fine as a king's;
Of good grape preserve was the crown,
Of sweet ribbon candy the strings!
    Her carriage, 'twould seem,
    Was all of ice cream;
    Her horses, O my!
    Each one a cold pie!

Nursery Friends from France

Now her husband, Mister Gimblette,
Wore a fine white cheese on his head;
And their daughter, sweet Charlotte Russe,
Had a nose of cherry jam red!
    Her best party gown
    Had bands up and down,
    Festoons made with art,
    Of apricot tart!

Curled and frizz'd, young Prince Lemonade
Came in style to sue for her hand;
Hair all garnished with marmalade,
Trimmed with gems of baked apples grand!
    The crown on his head
    Was cookies, 'tis said.
    He bore as bouquet,
    A fine raisin spray!

Nursery Friends
from France

His strong fiery guards made one quake;
They were pickles and peppers hot;
Oh, of onions sharp were their swords,
From their guns 'twas mustard they shot!
On her choc'late throne
Fair Charlotte sat down;
Her pockets, they say,
Streamed forth sweets all day!

Un poco allegro

Il é-tait un' da-me Tar-ti-ne, Dans un beau pa-lais de beurr'
There was once a dame called Tar-tine,— Had a but-ter pal-ace 'tis

frais, Les mu-raill's é-taient de fa-ri-ne, Le par-quet é-tait de cro-
said, Oh, its walls were all of white flour,— And its floors were crisp gin-ger-

quets, Sa chambre à cou-cher Étaient d'échau-dés, Son lit de bis-cuit: C'est fort son la nuit.
bread, Un-less I mis-take, Her bed-room was cake, She slept ev'-ry night on a bis-cuit light.

A Bold Brave Boy

I passed by a wood one day,
    'Twas where the cuckoos stay—
    'Twas where the cuckoos stay;
And in their pretty song they say:
    "Cuckoo! cuckoo! cuckoo! cuckoo!"
But I—I thought those cuckoos said:
    "Cook you! Cook you! Cook you! Cook you!"
And from that place I fled, fled, fled, fled,—
    I straightway fled away!

I passed by a pond one day,
    'Twas where young ducklings play—
    'Twas where young ducklings play;
And in their simple song they say:
    "Quack quack! quack quack! quack quack! quack quack!"
But I—I thought those ducklings said:
    "Whack Jack! whack whack! whack whack! whack whack!"
And from that place I fled, fled, fled, fled,—
    I straightway fled away!

I passed by a home one day,
    'Twas where sweet music rang—
    'Twas where sweet music rang;
And softly thus a good dame sang:
    "Bye-bye! bye-bye! bye-bye! bye-bye!"
But I—I thought that good dame said:
    "Bite boy! bite boy! bite boy! bite boy!"
And from that place I fled, fled, fled, fled,—
    I straightway fled away!

Sir, What Have You Seen?

Sir, what have you seen?
Dame, I've seen a sight!
   Saw an ox lift his legs
   Dancing lightly on eggs,
Never breaking one!
What a fib, my son!

Sir, what have you seen?
Dame, I've seen a sight!
   Saw a frog in the sun—
   With a distaff she spun,
Getting rich by a ditch!
What a fib, my son!

Sir, what have you seen?
Dame, I've seen a sight!
   Saw a fly do tricks,
   With paving bricks
On his nose, just for fun!
What a fib, my son!

Cadet Rousselle

Cadet Rousselle has houses three,
But none that has a roof, Ah, me!
Therein he lets the swallows dwell.
What say you of Cadet Rousselle?
    Oh! Oh!
    Oh, 'tis quite so!
Cadet Rousselle's a fine fellow!

Cadet Rousselle has three good coats,
One paper one, on which he dotes.
He wears his paper coat, you know,
Whene'er it storms with hail or snow!
    Oh! Oh!
    Oh, 'tis quite so!
Cadet Rousselle's a fine fellow!

Cadet Rousselle has three old hats,
Two ugly round ones black as bats;
The third's three-cornered, so 'tis said,—
It took its shape straight from his head!
     Oh! Oh!
    Oh, 'tis quite so!
Cadet Rousselle's a fine fellow!

Cadet Rousselle has three old shoes;
Two for his feet he needs must use;
The third one has no sole whate'er,—
That one he gives his sweet to wear!
     Oh! Oh!
    Oh, 'tis quite so!
Cadet Rousselle's a fine fellow!

Cadet Rousselle has three fine cats;
They never go a-catching rats!
The third, without a candle, mark!
Climbs to the attic in the dark!
      Oh! Oh!
    Oh, 'tis quite so!
Cadet Rousselle's a fine fellow!

Cadet Rousselle's three dogs beware!
One hunts the rabbit, one hunts hare.
The third whene'er he's called, they say,
Doth straightway run the other way!
      Oh! Oh!
    Oh, 'tis quite so!
Cadet Rousselle's a fine fellow!

Cadet Rousselle, a sword has he,
'Tis long, but rusty as can be;
He never seeks a quarrel then,
Save with a sparrow or a wren!
　　　Oh! Oh!
　　　Oh, 'tis quite so!
Cadet Rousselle's a fine fellow!

Cadet Rousselle has pennies three
Wherewith to pay his debts, you see.
He shows how he can pay and then
Puts in his purse those coins again!
　　　Oh! Oh!
　　　Oh, 'tis quite so!
Cadet Rousselle's a fine fellow!

Cadet Rousselle has three eyes, too,
One looks toward *Caen; one toward *Bayeux;
The third,—no man has guessed it yet,
The third is what but his lorgnette!
>   Oh! Oh!
> Oh, 'tis quite so!
Cadet Rouselle's a fine fellow!

*Caen and Bayeux are two quaint old towns in Normandy. Caen possesses two beautiful Norman abbeys nearly nine hundred years old. One was built by William the Conqueror, the sturdy old Norman who sailed across the English Channel and conquered England in the year 1066. The other was built by his wife, Mathilda.

Bayeux is most interesting because it possesses in a little house near the cathedral a famous piece of embroidery, called the Bayeux tapestry, which gives the entire story of the Norman Conquest, with Harold, the Saxon hero, William the Norman, and all their men outlined by needlework in the queerest, most angular figures. This piece of embroidery is a narrow strip, so long that it takes an hour to walk its length and examine the whole of it.

Caen and Bayeux are still among the most famous towns of Normandy.

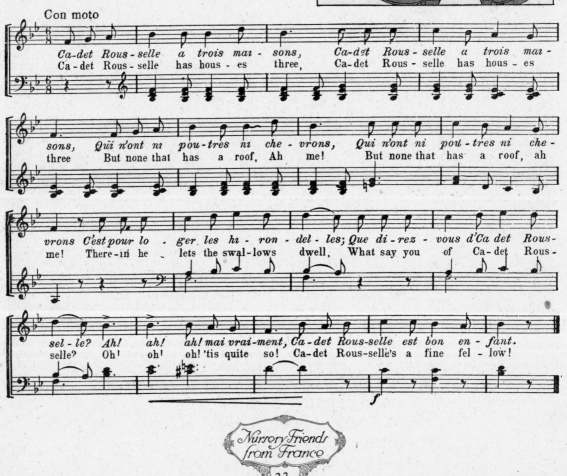

Con moto

Ca-det Rous-selle a trois mai-sons, Ca-det Rous-selle a trois mai-
Ca-det Rous-selle has hous-es three, Ca-det Rous-selle has hous-es

sons, Qui n'ont ni pou-tres ni che-vrons, Qui n'ont ni pou-tres ni che-
three But none that has a roof, Ah me! But none that has a roof, ah

vrons C'est pour lo-ger les hi-ron-del-les; Que di-rez-vous d'Ca-det Rous-
me! There-in he lets the swal-lows dwell, What say you of Ca-det Rous-

sel-le? Ah! ah! ah! mai vrai-ment, Ca-det Rous-selle est bon en-fant.
selle? Oh! oh! oh! 'tis quite so! Ca-det Rous-selle's a fine fel-low!

Ho, Pretty Dames

Ho, pretty dames, where are you going, pray?
Shoemaker fair, we're out to walk today.
Ho, pretty dames, you'll wear out your fine shoes!
Shoemaker fair, then mend them if you choose.
Ho, pretty dames, who'll pay me for them, pray?
Shoemaker fair, the one you catch shall pay!

These pretty dames are in the costume of the time of the Emperor Napoleon (1804-1815).

Mr. Punch

Booh! see who's here!
   Punchinello,
     My Ma'mselle-O!
Booh! see who's here!
'Tis good Mr. Punch who's here!

   Oddly he's made,
   But he'll do you no wrong!
   He only hopes
   To sing for you a song!

Booh! see who's here!
    Punchinello,
      My Ma'mselle-O!
Booh! see who's here!
'Tis good Mr. Punch who's here!

    Joyous all day,
    He loves to skip and dance;
    To sing at play,
    To balance and to prance.

Booh! see who's here!
    Punchinello,
      My Ma'mselle-O!
Booh! see who's here!
'Tis good Mr. Punch who's here!

    Crowds shout and laugh,
    When he humps up his back,
    Plays monkey tricks,
    And goes strut, strut, good lack!

Booh! see who's here!
    Punchinello,
      My Ma'mselle-O!
Booh! see who's here!
'Tis good Mr. Punch who's here!

By the Shining Moonlight

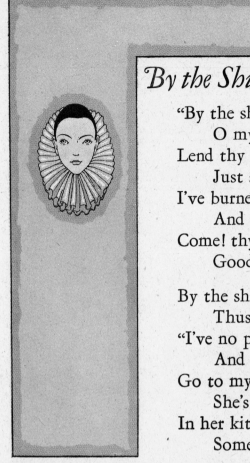

"By the shining moonlight,
  O my friend, Pierrot,
Lend thy pen for writing
  Just a word below.
I've burned out my candle,
  And my fire's out too;
Come! thy door pray open!
  Goodness sake, now do!"

By the shining moonlight,
  Thus friend Pierrot said:
"I've no pen to lend you,
  And I've gone to bed.
Go to my next neighbor's,
  She's at home tonight,—
In her kitchen—look you!
  Some one strikes a light!"

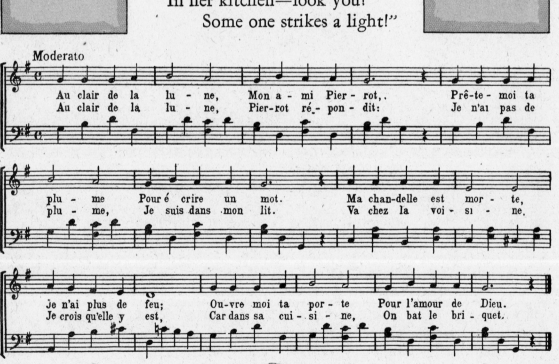

Au clair de la lu - ne, Mon a - mi Pier - rot,. Prê - te - moi ta
Au clair de la lu - ne, Pier - rot ré - pon - dit: Je n'ai pas de

plu - me Pour é crire un mot. Ma chan-delle est mor - te,
plu - me, Je suis dans mon lit. Va chez la voi - si - ne.

Je n'ai plus de feu; Ou-vre moi ta por - te Pour l'amour de Dieu.
Je crois qu'elle y est, Car dans sa cui - si - ne, On bat le bri - quet.

Harlequin

Harlequin his shop is holding
Under that great parasol;
See, he draws a crowd of people,
Come to buy things at his stall.
    Yes, Mister Po,
    Yes, Mister lee,
    Yes, Mister shee,
    Yes, Mister nell,
    Yes, Mister Po-li-chi-nelle!*

Harlequin sells sticks of lic'rice
Worth more than your stick, 'tis said;
And less noisy than you surely,
Are his men of gingerbread!
    Yes, Mister Po,
    Yes, Mister lee,
    Yes, Mister shee,
    Yes, Mister nell,
    Yes, Mister Po-li-chi-nelle!

*Polichinelle is the French name for Punch.

Little Marionettes

They do so, so, so,
    Little marionettes, Oho!
They do so, so, so,
    Turn three times and then they go!
      Au revoir!

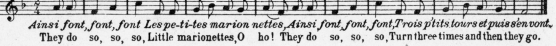

Ainsi font, font, font Les pe-ti-tes marion nettes, Ainsi font, font, font, Trois p'tits tours et puis s'en vont.
They do so, so, so, Little marionettes, O ho! They do so, so, so, Turn three times and then they go.

This is a game like pat-a-cake for young children. Both hands are held up and kept turning in singing, "They do so, so, so," and for the two lines following, to show how the marionettes dance. With the last line, "Turn three times and then they go," the hands are brought together in front, and rolled over each other three times, then spread out far apart, as in a farewell bow, with the word, au revoir!

Coqueliquette and Coquelicot

Farni Plump's young daughter bright,
Big and fat, but most polite,
    Coq'liquette,—
He did wed her to Pierrot;
Coq'liquette and Coq'licot.

His gift to her, now if you please,
Was some butter, bread and cheese,
    Coq'liquette,—
And some salt in a sabot;
Coq'liquette and Coq'licot.

The Notary was Bow-Legs there,
Mister One-Eye was the Mayor,
    Coq'liquette,—
Groom's best man was Pigeon-toe;
Coq'liquette and Coq'licot.

In Our Village

In our village
There's a learned advocate;
Three young women came to him,
To settle their debate.
 Skip now, advocate, you ninny!
 Skip you, skip you, skip you, advocate!

The poor advocate
Was taken by surprise,
To have studied for so long,
And never grown more wise!
 Skip now, advocate, you ninny!
 Skip you, skip you, skip you, advocate!

These peasants are in costumes from Brittany, one of the few provinces in France where many of the peasants continue to wear their costumes and have not replaced them with modern dress.

Happy Journey, Dear Dumollet!

Happy journey, dear Dumollay!
Off to St. Malo sail safely away!
Happy journey, dear Dumollay!
And if you like us, come back some fine day!

There, with your hands in your pockets, you'll see,
Wise men and simpletons pass, not a few;
Straight men and bandy-legged, crooked of knee,
But,—nary one with such fine legs as you!

Happy journey, dear Dumollay!
Off to St. Malo sail safely away!
Happy journey, dear Dumollay!
And if you like us, come back some fine day!

There sly young fellows will play waggish tricks;
Rogues! They will laugh at you under your nose!
Look out for spaniels and poodle-dogs, too,
Lest they come rubbing against your new hose!

St. Malo was a very nice place indeed for Mr. Dumollet to be setting out for. It is an old walled city on the sea in Brittany with huge old towers at its gates. Before the walls lies a fine stretch of beach, where all sorts of people promenade in summer. Off the shore are little islands of huge, gray, granite rocks, and on the blue sea may always be seen beautiful sailing vessels.

Nursery Friends from France

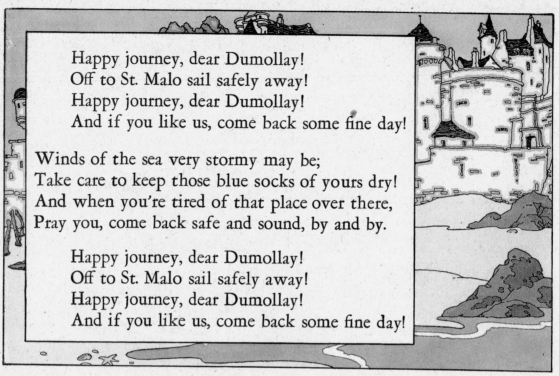

Happy journey, dear Dumollay!
Off to St. Malo sail safely away!
Happy journey, dear Dumollay!
And if you like us, come back some fine day!

Winds of the sea very stormy may be;
Take care to keep those blue socks of yours dry!
And when you're tired of that place over there,
Pray you, come back safe and sound, by and by.

Happy journey, dear Dumollay!
Off to St. Malo sail safely away!
Happy journey, dear Dumollay!
And if you like us, come back some fine day!

REFRAIN. Un poco allegro

Bon voy-a - ge Cher Du-mol- let, A Saint Ma- lo dé - bar-ques sans nau-
Hap- py jour-ney, dear Du-mol- let, Off to St. Ma- lo sail safe- ly a-

fra - ge; Bon voy-a - ge, cher Du-mol- let, Et re - ve-nez si le pa-ys vous plait.
way.___ Hap-py jour-ney, dear Du-mol- let, And if you like us come back some fine day.

Là vous ver-rez, les deux mains dans les po - ches Al- ler ve - nir des sa-ges et des
There with your hands in your pock-ets you'll see___ Wise men and sim-ple-tons pass not a

fous, Des gens bien faits, des tor tus des ban cro-ches, Nul ne se - ra jam bé si bien que vous.
few, Straight men and ban-dy legged crook-ed of knee,___ But na-ry one with such fine legs as you.

There is a Little Grenadier

There is a little grenadier
  With rosy cheek and tan:
He wears his bonnet on one ear
  Like any soldier man.
Ho, shoulder arms, and sword at side!
He's marching with a soldier's stride!
  Rum-tum-tee-tum-tum,
  Beat of the drum.
See there the guardsmen now advance.
Forward, ye bold grenadiers of France.
Advance, ye grenadiers! Advance!

Dame Michelle

It is Dame Michelle,
Who has just lost her cat,
And from her window cries:
"Pray who will bring him back?"
'Tis comrade Lustucru,
Who says: "Now don't booh hooh!
Come, come, good Dame Michelle,
Your cat's not lost to you!"

It is Dame Michelle,
Who cries out once again:
"Oh, is my cat not lost?
You must have found him then!"
'Tis comrade Lustucru,
Who says to her, "Quite true!
If you will pay the price,
I'll bring him back to you!"

It is Dame Michelle,
Who begs the rogue like this:
"Oh, bring me back my cat,
And I'll give you a kiss!"
"He's hunting in my barn
For rats," cries Lustucru,
"Armed with his little sword,
And wooden sabre, too!"

Allegretto

C'est la mér' Mi-chel qui a per-du son chat, Qui cri' par la fe-
C'est la mér' Mi-chel qui lui a de-man-dé: Mon chat n'est pas per-
Et la mér' Mi-chel lui dit: C'est dé-ci-dé, Si vous ren-dez mon

nêtre qu'est-ce-qui le lui ren-dra C'est l'comp ér' Lus-tu-cru qui
du! vous l'a-vez donc trou-vé? C'est l'comp ér' Lus-tu-cru qui
chat, 'vous au-rez un bai-ser. Il est dans mon gre-nier, qui

lui a ré-pon-du: Al-lez, la mer' Mi-chel, vot' chat n'est pas per-du.
lui a ré-pon-du: Don-nez un' re-com-pense, il vous se-ra ren-du.
fait la chasse aux rats, Av-ec sa-p'tite ép-ée et son sa-bre de bois.

A less interesting, but more common ending, in place of the last four lines, is this: 'Tis rascal Lustucru, who says, "That price won't do! I called your cat a hare, and sold him for a sou!"

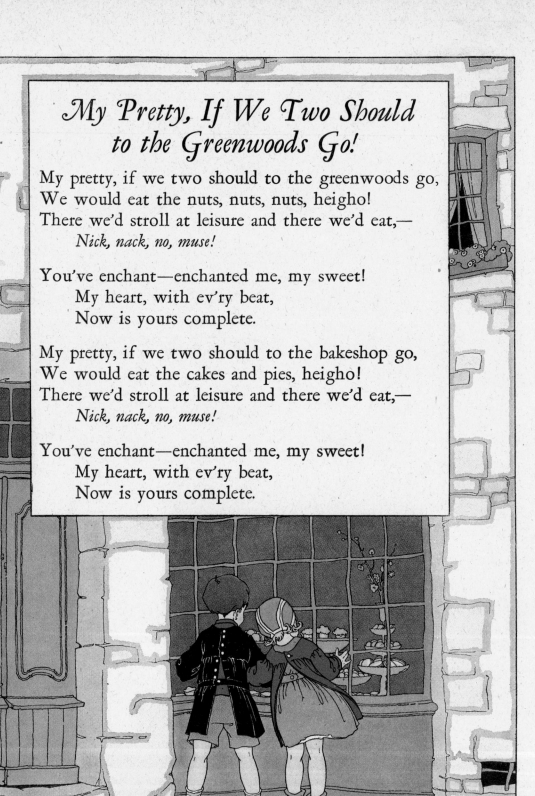

My Pretty, If We Two Should to the Greenwoods Go!

My pretty, if we two should to the greenwoods go,
We would eat the nuts, nuts, nuts, heigho!
There we'd stroll at leisure and there we'd eat,—
Nick, nack, no, muse!

You've enchant—enchanted me, my sweet!
My heart, with ev'ry beat,
Now is yours complete.

My pretty, if we two should to the bakeshop go,
We would eat the cakes and pies, heigho!
There we'd stroll at leisure and there we'd eat,—
Nick, nack, no, muse!

You've enchant—enchanted me, my sweet!
My heart, with ev'ry beat,
Now is yours complete.

My pretty, if we two should to a garden go,
We would sing all day with a ho! heigho!
All the flowers abloom with our songs we'd greet,—
   Nick, nack, no, muse!

You've enchant—enchanted me, my sweet!
   My heart, with ev'ry beat,
   Now is yours complete.

My pretty, if we two should to the river go,
We would watch the ducklings swim, heigho!
There at leisure watch how they ply their feet,—
   Nick, nack, no, muse!

You've enchant—enchanted me, my sweet!
   My heart, with ev'ry beat,
   Now is yours complete.

Good Day, Pretty Rosina

Good day, pretty Rosina!
      Pray now, how do you do?
Ah, but you make such faces,—
      Tell me, what's wrong with you!

'Tis, O alack! that my friend's gone away!
      That's what is making,—
      That's what is making,—
'Tis, O alack! that my friend's gone away!
That's what is making me sad today!

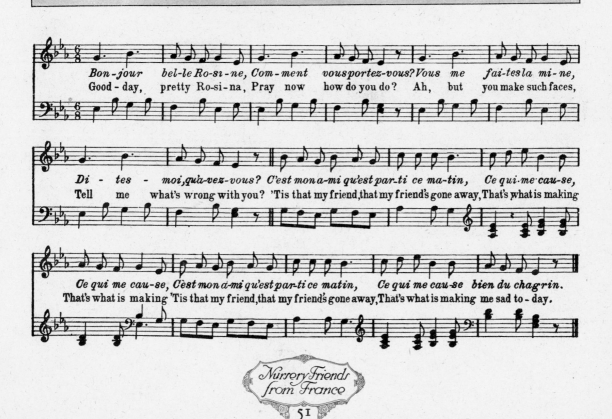

Bon-jour bel-le Ro-si-ne, Com-ment vous portez-vous? Vous me fai-tes la mi-ne,
Good-day, pretty Ro-si-na, Pray now how do you do? Ah, but you make such faces,

Di - tes - moi, qu'a-vez-vous? C'est mon a-mi qu'est par-ti ce ma-tin, Ce qui me cau-se,
Tell me what's wrong with you? 'Tis that my friend, that my friend's gone away, That's what is making

Ce qui me cau-se, C'est mon a-mi qu'est par-ti ce matin, Ce qui me cau-se bien du chagrin.
That's what is making 'Tis that my friend, that my friend's gone away, That's what is making me sad to - day.

Nursery Friends from France

On the Bridge of Avignon

On the bridge of Avignon,
There they're dancing! There they're dancing!
On the bridge of Avignon,
There they're dancing in a ring!
    Gentlemen do this way;
    Then again do this way!

On the bridge of Avignon,
There they're dancing! There they're dancing!
On the bridge of Avignon,
There they're dancing in a ring!
    Ladies all do this way;
    Then again do this way!

Allegretto.

Sur le pont d'A-vi-gnon L'on y dan-se, L'on y dan-se, Sur le pont d'A-vi-gnon

Avignon is a beautiful city on the banks of the river Rhone in southern France. It is so very old that it was an important town nearly two thousand years ago, in the days when France was called Gaul, and was owned by the Romans. There is to this day an interesting old bridge in Avignon, where doubtless

On the bridge of Avignon,
There they're dancing! There they're dancing!
On the bridge of Avignon,
There they're dancing in a ring!
    Nursemaids all do this way;
    Then again do this way!

On the bridge of Avignon,
There they're dancing! There they're dancing!
On the bridge of Avignon,
There they're dancing in a ring!
    Organ-men do this way;
    Then again do this way!

L'on y dan - se tout en rond. Les mes-sieurs font comme ça. Puis en - core font cómme çà.

generations of lords and ladies, organ-men and nursemaids, have danced to their hearts' content. This interesting old bridge still stands there, and every year the people of Avignon hold a festival and gather on the bridge to dance and sing this old song.

Nursery Friends from France

53

My Father's Given a Man to Me

My father's giv'n a man to me,
    Good lack that man!
    That little man!
One tiny leaf his clothes might be.
    Good lack that man!
    Great heav'ns how wee!

Standing on that small plate is he,
    Good lack that man!
    That little man!
"Ha!" thinks the cat, "a mouse I see!"
    Good lack that man!
    Great heav'ns how wee!

Now! she's run off with him, Ah me!
    Good lack that man!
    That little man!
O chase her! Chase her! Set him free!
    Good lack that man!
    Great heav'ns how wee!

Mon pèr' m'a don-né un ma-ri, Mon Dieu! quel homm', quel pe-tit
My fa-ther's giv'n a man to me, Good lack! that man, that lit-tle

hom-me. D'u-ne feuille on fit son ha-bit, Mon Dieu! quel homm', qu'il est pe-tit!
man!   One ti-ny   leaf his clothes might be, Good lack that man,   Great heav'ns, how wee!

There Was Once a Schooner

Oh, there was once a schooner
 With thirty sailors free,
With thirty sailor men on the shore of Belle Isle,
With thirty sailor men down beside the sea!

Now what's the trouble, pretty?
 What makes you cry,—Ah me!
What makes you cry so much on the shore of Belle Isle?
What makes you cry so much down beside the sea?

Do you weep for your father,
    Or mother,—can it be?
Or for some cousin dear on the shore of Belle Isle,
Or for some cousin dear down beside the sea?

    I'm weeping for a schooner
    With sails set out to sea,
With sails set to the wind on the shore of Belle Isle,
With sails set to the wind down beside the sea!

    It's gone away for trading,
    And carried off from me
My sweetheart, sweetheart, sweet, on the shore of Belle Isle,
My sweetheart, sweetheart, sweet, down beside the sea!

Belle Isle is an island off the south coast of Brittany.

Margoton Goes to the Well

Margoton takes her jug;
O to the well she's gone.
The well's deep! She falls in!
Alas, what has she done!
"Ai! Ai! Ai! Ai!"
So says Margoton.

The well's deep! She falls in!
Alas, what has she done!
Ah, lo! three handsome youths
Come passing by anon.
"Ai! Ai! Ai! Ai!"
So says Margoton.

Ah, lo! three handsome youths
Come passing by anon.
"What will you give us, pray,
To pull you out?" cries one.
"Ai! Ai! Ai! Ai!"
So says Margoton.

"What will you give us, pray,
To pull you out?" cries one.
"A kiss as good as gold
To ev'ry mother's son
Ai! Ai! Ai! Ai!"
So says Margoton.

Un peu Allegro

Mar-go-ton va-t-a l'iau A-vec-que son cru chon, Mar-go-ton
Mar-go-ton takes her jug O to the well she's gone. Mar-go-ton

va-t-a l'iau A-vec-que son cru-chon. La fontaine é - tait
takes her jug O to the well she's gone. The well's deep, she falls

creuse, Elle est tombée au fond: Aïe, aïe, aïe, aïe, se dit Mar-go-ton.
in A-las what has she done? "Ai! Ai! Ai! Ai!" So says Mar-go-ton.

Nursery Friends from France

To Paree, to Paree

To Paree, to Paree,
On a fine gray pony wee!

To Verdun, to Verdun,
On a little pony brown!

To Cambrai, to Cambrai,
On a little pony bay!

Now come back, now come back,
On a little pony black!

Slow, slow,   slow, slow,
Trot, trot,   trot, trot,
And gallop! And gallop!

A Pa - ris, à Pa - ris, Sur un pe - tit che - val gris.
A Ver - dun, à Ver - dun, Sur un pe - tit che - val brun.
A Cam - brai, à Cam - brai, Sur un pe - tit che - val bai.
Re - ve - nons au ma - noir Sur un pe - tit che - val noir.

SPEAK:
Au pas! Au pas! Au trot! Au trot! Au galop! Au galop!

Verdun is a fortified town in the north of France. Though battered by months of cannon fire, it withstood one of the greatest assaults in history in 1914 during the War of the Nations, when the Germans marched toward Paris. Cambrai is another old town of Northern France, with its ancient walls and towers still standing.

Miller, You Sleep

Miller, you sleep,
And your mill
Goes too quickly!
Miller, you sleep,
And your mill
Goes too fast!

Meu-nier, tu-dors, Ton mou-lin va trop vi-te, Meu-nier, tu-dors, Ton mou-lin va trop fort.

Bye-lo, Baby, Bye!

Bye-lo, baby, bye,
Hush thee now and do not cry!
There's a hen all white,
In the barn tonight!
She is going to make cocoa
For the baby who goes bye-lo.
Bye-lo, my little chickie,
Bye-lo, my chickie-o!

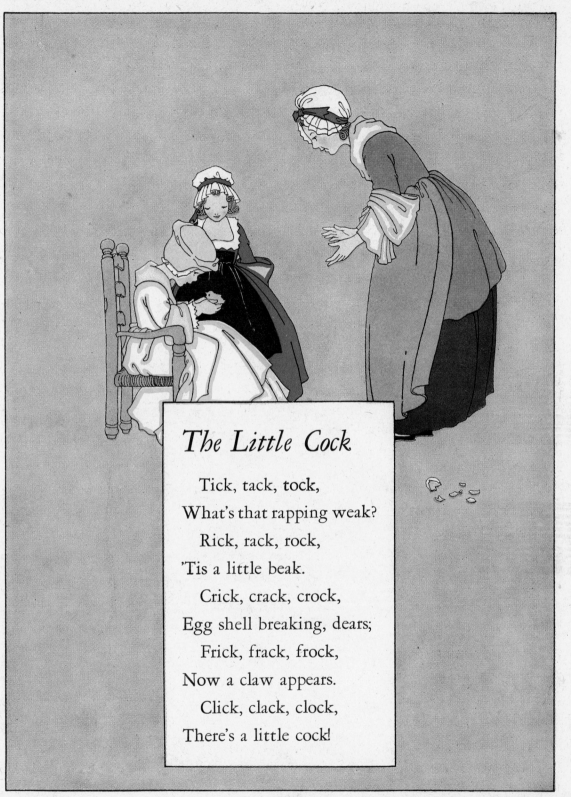

The Little Cock

Tick, tack, tock,
What's that rapping weak?
Rick, rack, rock,
'Tis a little beak.
Crick, crack, crock,
Egg shell breaking, dears;
Frick, frack, frock,
Now a claw appears.
Click, clack, clock,
There's a little cock!

These figures were suggested by a painting called "Grace Before Meat," by Jean-Baptiste-François Chardin (1699-1779) the greatest of French artists in the painting of scenes from home life. His work, however, remained little noticed in his own day, when people loved best the fanciful figures of Watteau and Boucher.

Long Live Wooden Shoes

It was Anne of Brittany,
    In her wooden shoes;
Home from her rich lands came she,
In wooden shoes, O-tira-lee!
    Ah! Ah! Ah!
Long live wooden shoes!

This figure is taken from an ancient portrait of Anne of Brittany found in a prayer book belonging to the queen.

Nursery Friends from France

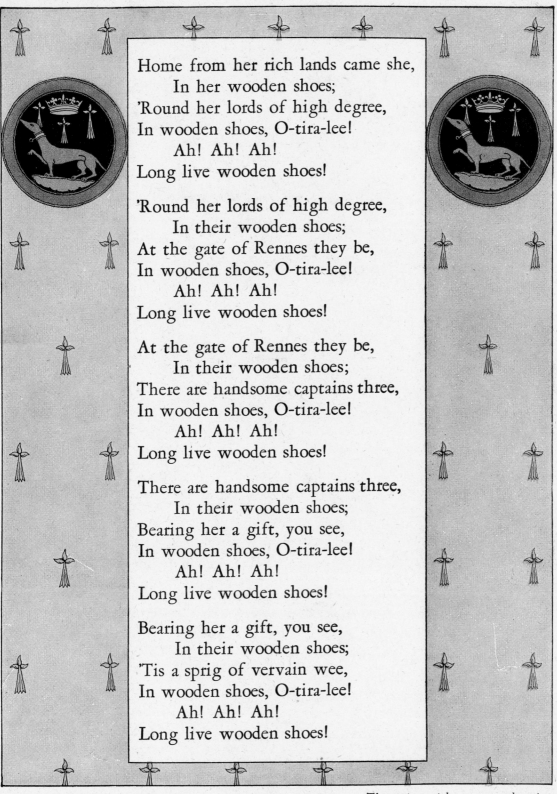

Home from her rich lands came she,
      In her wooden shoes;
'Round her lords of high degree,
In wooden shoes, O-tira-lee!
      Ah! Ah! Ah!
Long live wooden shoes!

'Round her lords of high degree,
      In their wooden shoes;
At the gate of Rennes they be,
In wooden shoes, O-tira-lee!
      Ah! Ah! Ah!
Long live wooden shoes!

At the gate of Rennes they be,
      In their wooden shoes;
There are handsome captains three,
In wooden shoes, O-tira-lee!
      Ah! Ah! Ah!
Long live wooden shoes!

There are handsome captains three,
      In their wooden shoes;
Bearing her a gift, you see,
In wooden shoes, O-tira-lee!
      Ah! Ah! Ah!
Long live wooden shoes!

Bearing her a gift, you see,
      In their wooden shoes;
'Tis a sprig of vervain wee,
In wooden shoes, O-tira-lee!
      Ah! Ah! Ah!
Long live wooden shoes!

Nursery Friends
from France

The ermine, with a crown and ermine
tails above, was the coat of arms of
Anne of Brittany.

'Tis a sprig of vervain wee,
    In their wooden shoes;
"If it blooms a queen you'll be,
In wooden shoes, O-tira-lee!"
    Ah! Ah! Ah!
Long live wooden shoes!

"If it blooms a queen you'll be,
    In your wooden shoes!"
It has bloomed, that vervain wee,
In wooden shoes, O-tira-lee!
    Ah! Ah! Ah!
Long live wooden shoes!

It has bloomed, that vervain wee,
    In her wooden shoes!
Wedding France's king is she,
In wooden shoes, O-tira-lee!
    Ah! Ah! Ah!
Long live wooden shoes!

Wedding France's king is she,
    In her wooden shoes!
Bretons lose their fair ladye,
In wooden shoes, O-tira-lee!
    Ah! Ah! Ah!
Long live wooden shoes!

The young Duchess Anne, heiress of the fair province of Brittany, was carried off from under the very nose of old Maximilian of Austria, who wished to gain all her rich lands by wedding her, and married to the youth, Charles VIII of France, in 1491, thus finally uniting the duchy of Brittany to France. All through the finest chateaux of France, memories of her, statues, pictures, and emblems of her linger to this day.

Rennes was once the capital of Brittany, and the Dukes of Brittany were crowned there. It still has its old walls, towers and gates of the middle ages, a picturesque spot in the most picturesque province of France.

Allegro

C'é-tait An - ne de Bre-ta-gne A-vec ses sa-bots, C'é - tait An - ne
It was Anne of Brit-tan - y___ In her wood-en shoes, It was Anne of

de Bre-ta-gne A-vec ses sa-bots, Re - ve-nant de ses do-mai-nes
Brit-tan - y___ In her wood-en - shoes, Home from her rich lands came she, In

En sa-bots,mir-li-ton-tai-ne, Ah! Ah! Ah! Vi-vent les sa-bots de bois!
wood-en shoes, O ti-ra-lee, Ah! Ah! Ah! Long___ live wood-en shoes!

Nursery Friends
from France

67

Pretty Poppy, O My Ladies

I wandered all my garden through,
To pick rosemary and the rue;—
   Pretty poppy, Oh my ladies!
   Pretty poppy, fresh with dew!

I picked three sprays, but just so few,
When Nightingale to my hand flew,—
   Pretty poppy, Oh my ladies!
   Pretty poppy, fresh with dew!

He spoke three words in latin true,
He said, "Men are not worth a sou!"
   Pretty poppy, Oh my ladies,
   Pretty poppy, fresh with dew!

He said, "Men are not worth a sou!
And boys are worth as little, too!—"
   Pretty poppy, Oh my ladies!
   Pretty poppy, fresh with dew!

Of ladies nothing 'twas he knew,
"But girls," said he, "are fine, coo, coo!"
   Pretty poppy, Oh my ladies!
   Pretty poppy, fresh with dew!

Comrade, When I Start A-Dancing

Comrade, when I start a-dancing,
Don't you find my dance entrancing?
    Now we go here, now we go there,—
    Hi! it goes right well, my comrade!
    Now we go there, now we go here,—
    Hi! it goes right well, my dear!

Twist and turn! Come twirling after,—
Oh, I think I'll die with laughter!
    Now we go here, now we go there,—
    Hi! it goes right well, my comrade!
    Now we go there, now we go here,—
    Hi! it goes right well, my dear!

The King of Yvetot

There was a King of Yvetot,
But little known in story;
He snored right early, slept right late,
And what cared he for glory?
By simple John crowned one fine day,
In a plain cotton cap, his way,
    they say—
    Oh, ring a ding!
    O cheer, cheer, cheer!
    What a nice little King
    Is here, here, here!

He ate each day his four square meals,
In his thatched palace humble,
And 'stride a donkey, slow of heels,
He rode out, stumble, stumble.
With faith in all and trust profound,
He took but one guard on his round,—
        his hound—
    Oh, ring a ding!
    O cheer, cheer, cheer!
    What a nice little King
    Is here, here, here!

He had no wish to fight for land—
As neighbor he'd no flaw—
And best of kings, he gave command:
"Make merry—that's my law!"
Ah! while he lived 'tis not denied
His jolly good folk never sighed,
        nor cried—
    Oh, ring a ding!
    O cheer, cheer, cheer!
    What a nice little King
    Is here, here, here!

His portrait's even now preserved,
That prince with friendly grin;
Hung out as sign 't may be observed
Before a famous inn.
There oft on feast days shouts arise.
The crowd his kind face then espies,
    and cries:
      "Oh, ring a ding!
      O cheer, cheer, cheer!
      What a nice little King
      Is here, here, here!"

Yvetot is an old, old town in Normandy. From the fif-
teenth to the middle of the sixteenth centuries, the lords
of Yvetot bore the title King, and owed no service to the
Kings of France. It is by this very song, however, that the
little old town of Yvetot is best known to the world.

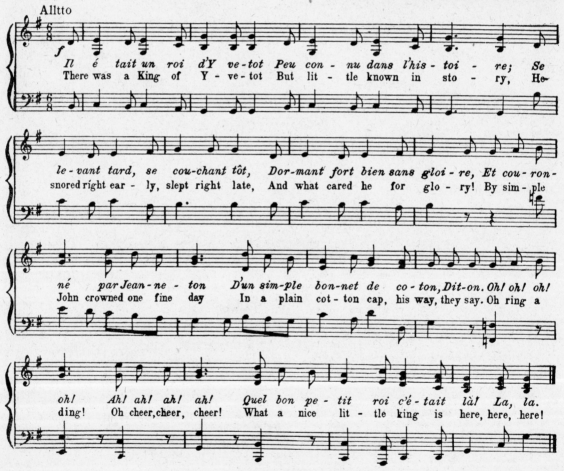

Alltto

Il é tait un roi d'Y ve-tot Peu con nu dans l'his-toi re; Se
There was a King of Y-ve-tot But lit-tle known in sto-ry, He-

le-vant tard, se cou-chant tôt, Dor-mant fort bien sans gloi-re, Et cou-ron-
snored right ear-ly, slept right late, And what cared he for glo-ry! By sim-ple

né par Jean-ne-ton D'un sim-ple bon-net de co-ton, Dit-on. Oh! oh! oh!
John crowned one fine day In a plain cot-ton cap, his way, they say. Oh ring a

oh! Ah! ah! ah! ah! Quel bon pe-tit roi c'é-tait là! La, la.
ding! Oh cheer, cheer, cheer! What a nice lit-tle king is here, here, here!

Little Christophe

I went to walk one day so fine
Down by the sea in bright sunshine.
Whom should I meet but small Christophe,
Dressed in his suit of gay silk stuff.
　　A pretty band of red
Made fine the hat upon his head.

Said I to him: "Why is it, pray,
You're all dressed up in this grand way?"
Little Christophe then raised his head;
"There's a grand fête in town," he said
　　"A party there's to be
At Uncle Michael's home, you see!"

What then should hap but at that time
His little dog played romp with mine.
Ah! Ah! Christophe to anger quick,—
He thought to give his dog a kick.
　　As he did, sad to tell,
He stubbed his toe and down he fell.

Said I to him: "Christophe, my friend,
'Twas only thus your wrath could end.
You're served quite right for acting so,
To wish to kick your dog, you know,
　　You've soiled your hat," I said,
"And lost your band of lovely red!"

La Palisse

Gentlemen, hark to the song
  Of the great Palisse,—pray do!
He'll delight you, I am sure,—
  If he only pleases you.
La Palisse was poor at birth;
  Ah! his early days were rough,
But he never lacked a thing,—
  Just as soon as he'd enough!

He was taught with greatest care,
  And was so polite, 'tis said,
That he ne'er put on his hat
  Without covering his head.
He was gentle, too, and kind,
  Like his father, wise and sage,
And was never, never cross,—
  Save when he was in a rage.

His hair was a lovely gold,
  And it shone bright as the sun;
He'd have been the best of men,—
  If he'd been the only one!
He had such a noble air
  That he pleased both high and low.
The King would have made him duke,
  If he'd chosen to do so!

He sometimes sailed in a boat,
    For at all times he was grand.
When he journeyed on the sea,
    He would never go by land!
He had servants rarely trained,
    Serving wondrous fine croquettes,
And they never left out eggs,
    When they made him omelettes!

He set out to run a race,
    In a tournament one day.
When he came before the King,
    He was not behind, they say!
As he rode a great black horse,
    All the maids thought him quite trim,
And 'twas there that he was seen
    By each one who looked at him!

When he wished to live in peace,
To the country he went down.
One would then have wasted time,
To have looked for him in town!
He was married to a maid,
And he loved her all his life.
On the day that they were wed,
He took her to be his wife.

Pas trop vite

Messieurs, vous plait-il d'ouir L'air du fameux La Pa lis - se? Il pour-ra vous
Gen - tle-men, hark to the song of the great Pa-lisse pray do,_____ He'll de-light you

ré-jou-ir Pour vu qu'il vous di-ver-tis - se. La Pa-lisse eut peu de bien Pour sou-
I am sure if he on-ly pleas-es you, La Pa-lisse was poor at birth, ah his

te-nir sa nais-san-ce, Mais il ne man-qua de rien Dés qu'il fut dans l'a-bon-dan-ce.
ear-ly days were rough___ But he nev-er lacked a thing Just as soon as he'd e - nough._

This beautiful lady is in the costume of
the days of Marie Antoinette, the unfor-
tunate queen of Louis XVI, who lost her
head in the days of the French Revolution,
when the people replaced the ancient kingdom with a republic.

Adventures

I'm a jolly little man,
And polite as you can see;
Oh, of candy, cake and jam
I'm as fond as I can be!
If you would give me some sweet,
Surely I'd know how to eat!
    'Twould be jubilee,—
        A treat!
    'Twould be jubilee!

Now it chances when small boys
Are gentle and wise,
They are given bon-bons and toys
And presents to prize.
When they're naughty, though, and bad,
'Tis a whip is giv'n each lad,—
    Oh, adventure of sighs,—
        Sad!
    Oh, adventure of sighs!

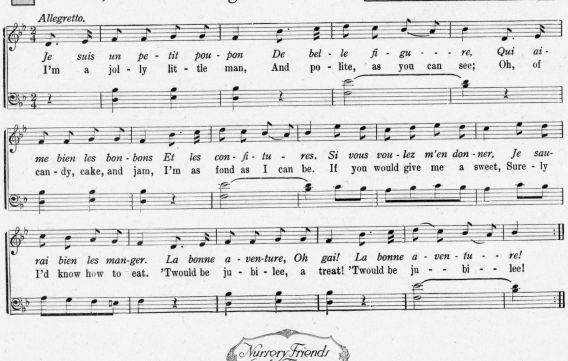

Allegretto.

Je suis un pe - tit pou - pon De bel - le fi - gu - - re, Qui ai -
I'm a jol - ly lit - tle man, And po - lite, as you can see; Oh, of

me bien les bon - bons Et les con - fi - tu - res. Si vous vou - lez m'en don - ner, Je sau -
can - dy, cake, and jam, I'm as fond as I can be. If you would give me a sweet, Sure - ly

rai bien les man - ger. La bonne a - ven - ture, Oh gai! La bonne a - ven - tu - - re!
I'd know how to eat. 'Twould be ju - bi - lee, a treat! 'Twould be ju - - bi - - lee!

The King of Sardinia

'Twas a King of old Sardinia,
Who was powerful bold of yore;
"Ho! I'll capture me the Sultan!"
One fine day he proudly swore.
  With a clap!—Hands behind you,
  And a clap, clap before.

He had ninety knaves for army,
And not even one man more,
And he found, on counting cannon,
That he had exactly four!
  With a clap!—Hands behind you,
  And clap, clap before!

Ah, he reached the mountains crying,
"How the grand moonlight doth pour!"
But just then he spied the Sultan—
"Run for life!" now he did roar!
  With a clap!—Hands behind you,
  And a clap, clap before!

Con moto

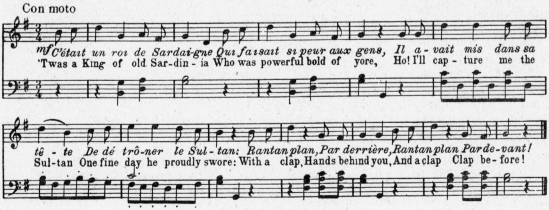

mf C'était un roi de Sardaigne Qui faisait si peur aux gens, Il a-vait mis dans sa
'Twas a King of old Sar-din-ia Who was powerful bold of yore, Ho! I'll cap-ture me the

tê-te De dé trô-ner le Sul-tan: Rantan plan, Par derrière, Rantan plan Par de-vant!
Sul-tan One fine day he proudly swore: With a clap, Hands behind you, And a clap Clap be-fore!

When Great Biron Wants to Dance

When great Biron wants to dance,
Bring him the best shoes in France!
  In your shoes so gay,
   Great Biron, dance away!

When great Biron wants to dance,
Bring him the best wig in France!
   His big wig
   For a jig.
  In your shoes so gay,
   Great Biron, dance away!

When great Biron wants to dance,
Bring him the best vest in France!
    His best vest,
    Star on breast;
    His big wig
    For a jig.
  In your shoes so gay,
  Great Biron, dance away!

When great Biron wants to dance,
Bring him the best pants in France!
    His dance pants
    For to prance;
    His best vest,
    Star on breast;
    His big wig
    For a jig.
  In your shoes so gay,
  Great Biron, dance away.

When great Biron wants to dance,
Bring him the best coat in France!
    Coat of note,
    Lace at throat;
    His dance pants
    For to prance;
    His best vest,
    Star on breast;
    His big wig
    For a jig.
  In your shoes so gay,
  Great Biron, dance away!

The Dukes of Biron were a famous, noble family of
France. In the year 1600 one of them was a stout
rebel against Henry IV.

Music-in-the-Air

Little gentle sir,
What can you do there?
Can you, can you play
Music-in-the-air,
  airy, airy, air?
Ah, ah, ah! What can you do there?

Little gentle sir,
What can you do there?
Can you, can you play
Music-on-the-flute,
  flutey, flutey, flute,
  airy, airy, air?
Ah, ah, ah! What can you do there?

Little gentle sir,
What can you do there?
Can you, can you play
Music-on-the-drum,
  drummy, drummy, drum,
  flutey, flutey, flute,
  airy, airy, air?
Ah, ah, ah! What can you do there?

Little gentle sir,
What can you do there?
Can you, can you play
Music-on-the-horn,
    horny, horny, horn,
    drummy, drummy, drum,
    flutey, flutey, flute,
    airy, airy, air?
Ah, ah, ah, What can you do there?

Little gentle sir,
What can you do there?
Can you, can you play
Music-on-the-harp,
    harpy, harpy, harp,
    horny, horny, horn,
    drummy, drummy, drum,
    flutey, flutey, flute,
    airy, airy, air?
Ah, ah, ah! What can you do there?

Little gentle sir,
What can you do there?
Can you, can you play
Music-on-the-viol,
  viol, viol, viol,
  harpy, harpy, harp,
  horny, horny, horn,
  drummy, drummy, drum,
  flutey, flutey, flute,
  airy, airy, air?
Ah, ah, ah! What can you do there?

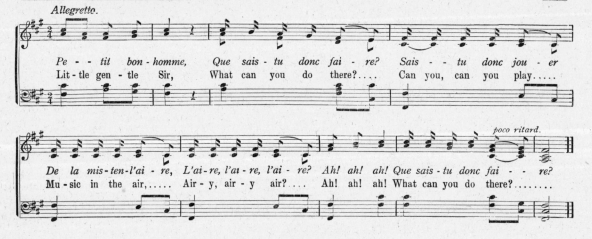

Allegretto.

Pe - - til bon - homme, Que sais - tu donc fai - re? Sais - - tu donc jou - er
Lit - tle gen - tle Sir, What can you do there?.... Can you, can you play.....

poco ritard.

De la mis - ten - l'ai - re, L'ai - re, l'ai - re, l'ai - re? Ah! ah! ah! Que sais - tu donc fai - - re?
Mu - sic in the air,..... Air - y, air - y air?.... Ah! ah! ah! What can you do there?........

I Would Tell You, Mother Dear

I would tell you, mother dear,
Why I sit a-crying here.
Papa's set me sums to do,
Like a great big man, boo hoo!
Good sweet candy any day
Is worth more than sums, I say.

Allegro

Ah! Vous di - rai je, ma - mam, Ce qui cau-se mon tour - ment!
I would tell you moth-er dear, Why I sit a cry-ing here!

Pa - pa veut que je rai - son - ne Comme u - ne gran - de per - son - ne;
Pa - pa's set me sums to do Like a great big man, boo hoo - ooh

Moi je dis que les bon - bons___ Va - lent mieux que la rai - son.
Good sweet can - dy an - y day___ Is worth more than sums I say.

These figures were suggested by a portrait of Madame Seriziat by J. L. David (1748-1825) which hangs in the Museum of the Louvre.

Nursery Friends from France

Our Donkey Got Up Early

Our donkey got up early,
  An hour before the day;
And with his belt and saddle,
  Took to the woods his way.

Ah, but he soon encountered
  Friend Wolf so lean and gray.
"I'll eat you like a cabbage,"
  His friend, the wolf, did say!

"Oh don't do that, good fellow!
  Instead, come with me, pray!
I'm going to a wedding;
  Believe me, 'twill be gay!"

He took best place at table,
  Upon that wedding day!
"Fair bride, I drink your health!'
  Politely he did bray.

Little Mousie Gray

We've caught you now at last,
  You little mousie gray;
We've caught you now at last,
  You shall not get away!

    Ah, but God made me to run,
      My gentle little girlies;
    God made me to run, you know,
      Let me go! Let me go!

Nay, nay, you came to steal,
  You little mousie gray;
Nay, nay, you came to steal
  Our breakast all away!

    I will steal your food no more,
      My gentle, little girlies;
    I will steal your food no more,
      I'll be good! I implore!

If you're sorry, you shall go,
  You little mousie gray:
See, your prison door now yields,
  Take the key to the fields!

Master Lark Took Mistress Finch

Master Lark took Mistress Finch
For to be his bride, tweet, tweet!
But it chanced the next day that
They had not a bite to eat.

> Ah, you lark,
> Sing tour-lou-ree-reet,
> My bird so sweet,
> No bite to eat!

There passed by a hare, 'tis said,
In one arm a loaf of bread;
But we've too much bread, indeed,—
'Tis of meat that we have need.

> Ah, you lark,
> Sing tour-lou-ree-reet,
> My bird so sweet,
> No bite to eat!

There passed by a crow alone,
In his beak a mutton bone;
But we've too much meat, indeed,—
'Tis of music we have need!

> Ah, you lark,
> Sing tour-lou-ree-reet,
> My bird so sweet,
> No bite to eat!

Passed a rat then, gaunt and thin,
In his arm a violin.
"At your service," said the Rat,
"If you've here no Mistress Cat!"

    Ah, you lark,
    Sing tour-lou-ree-reet,
    My bird so sweet,
    No bite to eat!

Enter! Enter, then and play,
Master of the dance, we pray!
Here, believe me, you're quite free;
Our cat's in the granary!

    Ah, you lark,
    Sing tour-lou-ree-reet,
    My bird so sweet,
    No bite to eat!

The Dance of the Pigs

When I was at home at Father's,—
    Youp, la la! Lolly rah!
I was guarding pigs all day,
    Youp, la lolly retto gay!

As I passed the meadows with them,—
    Youp, la la! Lolly rah!
Ho, my pigs all ran away!
    Youp, la lolly retto gay!

Said my little servant Peter,—
    Youp, la la! Lolly rah!
"I'll bring back those pigs, I say,"
    Youp, la lolly retto gay!

Peter took his merry bagpipe,—
    Youp, la la! Lolly rah!
On his bagpipe he did play,
    Youp, la lolly retto gay!

When they heard that bagpipe playing,—
    Youp, la, la! Lolly rah!
In that moment back came they,
    Youp, la lolly retto gay!

By their paws they took each other,—
    Youp, la la! Lolly rah!
All began to dance away,
    Youp, la lolly retto gay!

Only one old lady piggie,—
    Youp, la la! Lolly rah!
Would not skip one skip,—nay, nay!
    Youp, la lolly retto gay!

Fattest Mister Pig approached her,—
    Youp, la la! Lolly rah!
"Fair one, come and dance, I pray!'
    Youp, la lolly retto gay'

Then they made each other curtsies,—
    Youp, la la! Lolly rah!
High, sky-high they skipped away,
    Youp, la lolly retto gay!

Bye-lo-bye, Colas, Little Brother

Bye-lo-bye, Colas, little brother,
　Hush now,—come;
　I'll give you yum, yum!
Mamma's up above;
　She makes cake, my love.
Papa's down below,
　And he makes you cocoa!
Bye-lo-bye, Colas, little brother
　Hush now,—come;
　I'll give you yum, yum!

Allegretto.

Fais do - do, Co - las, mon p'tit Frè - re; Fais do - do, t'au - ras du lo -
Bye - lo - bye, Co - las, lit - tle broth - er, Hush now, come! I'll give you yum

lo; Ma - man est en haut Qui jait du gâ - teau, Pa - pa est en bas Qui fait du cho - co -
yum. Mam - ma's up a - bove, She makes cake, my love. Pa - pa's down be - low, And he makes you co -

lat: Fais do - do, Co - las, mon p'tit Frè - re, Fais do - do, t'au - ras du lo - lo.
coa. Bye - lo - bye, Co - las, lit - tle broth - er, Hush now, come! I'll give you yum yum.

Nursery Friends
from France

Nursery Friends from France

93

There Was Once a Huntsman Small

There was once a huntsman small,
He rode horseback on a cane;
Boldly he set forth to chase,
To chase may-bugs o'er the plain.
O tee tum tum
and tum tum tee,
and tee tum tum
and tum tum tee!

1. Il é-tait un pe-tit homm', A che-val sur un bâ-ton; Il s'en al-lait à la chass', A la
2. Quand il fut sur la mon-tagn', Il par-tit un coup d'ca-non; Il en eut si peur tout d'mêm', Qu'il tom-
3. Tout's les dam-es du vil-lag', Lui por-tè-rent des bon-bons. Je vous re-mer-ci', mes-dam's, De vous

When he reached the hunting place,
He heard roar! a cannon sound.
In a panic he fell flat
On his nose upon the ground.
    O tee tum tum
        and tum tum tee,
        and tee tum tum
            and tum tum tee!

From the village then came dames,
Bringing to him candy sweet.
"Thank you, ladies, I'm quite bold,
When there's candy I must eat."
    O tee tum tum
        and tum tum tee,
        and tee tum tum
            and tum tum tee!

chass' aux z'han - ne - tons, Et ti ton tain', et ti ton tain', Et ti ton ton, et ti ton tain'!
ba sur ses ta - lons; Et ti ton tain', et ti ton tain', Et ti ton ton, et ti ton tain'!
et de vos bon - bons, Et ti ton tain', et ti ton tain', Et ti ton ton, et ti ton tain'!

Nursery Friends from France

A-Fishing for Fresh Mussels

A-fishing for fresh mussels,
I wish no more to go, mamma!
A-fishing for fresh mussels,
I wish no more to go!

    They'll take my basket from me,—
    The bad boys of Marennes, mamma!
    They'll take my basket from me,—
    The bad boys of Marennes!

A-fishing for fresh mussels,
I wish no more to go, mamma!
A-fishing for fresh mussels,
I wish no more to go!

Oh, if they catch and hold me,
Say, are they then good boys, mamma?
Oh, if they catch and hold me,
Say, are they then good boys?

A-fishing for fresh mussels,
I wish no more to go, mamma!
A-fishing for fresh mussels,
I wish no more to go!

If ocean's fair and shiny,
I'll wear my best white shoes, mamma!
If ocean's fair and shiny,
I'll wear my best white shoes!

A-fishing for fresh mussels,
I wish no more to go, mamma!
A-fishing for fresh mussels,
I wish no more to go!

But if the weather's rainy,
I'll wear old wooden shoes, mamma!
But if the weather's rainy,
I'll wear old wooden shoes!

A-fishing for fresh mussels,
I wish no more to go, mamma!
A-fishing for fresh mussels,
I wish no more to go!

Break Your Bread, Mary

Break your bread, Mary;
Break your bread, Mary;
Break your bread in the saucer!
Break your bread, Mary;
Break your bread, Mary;
Break your bread in the milk!
We will go on Sunday
To the white house, honey;
You in nankeen,
I in bombazine,
Both in shoes of silk!

Allegretto

Tremp' ton pain, Ma - rie, Tremp' ton pain, Ma - rie, Tremp' ton pain dans la
sau - ce, Tremp' ton pain, Ma-rie, Tremp' ton pain, Ma-rie, Tremp' ton pain dans le

Break your bread, Mary;
   Break your bread, Mary;
      Break your bread in the saucer!
Break your bread, Mary;
   Break your bread, Mary;
      Break your bread in the milk!
   All along the Seine—O!
   We'll go to Suresne—O!
     Sit on green grass,
     Eat small cakes, lass,
  And watch the ships that pass.

vin.   Nous i-rons di-man-che   A la mai-son blan-che

Toi-z-en Nan-kin, Moi-z-en ba-zin, Tous deux en es-car-pins.

Nursery Friends from France

'Tis Dames of Paris

'Tis dames of Paris, so they say,
Who clean their houses all the day,—
  My fine ribbon gray!
  Oh, my fine ribbon yellow!
  My pretty gray yellow, my gray,
  My fine yellow ribbon so gay!

From bed to table sweep away,
From table to the door, hooray,—
  My fine ribbon gray!
  Oh, my fine ribbon yellow!
  My pretty gray yellow, my gray,
  My fine yellow ribbon so gay!

Nursery Friends
from France

The Little Seamstress

Far away in Paris a little seamstress sews,
Takes such tiny stitches none ever shows.
Ne'er did I see such teeny, tiny stitches;
    Ne'er did I see
    Stitches so wee!

She hems linen for the notary so wary,
And takes work to Monsieur Apothecary.
Ne'er did I see such teeny, tiny stitches;
    Ne'er did I see
    Stitches so wee!

"Seamstress, how much is what you have to sell me?"
"Two sous and a half. Is that dear, pray tell me?"
Ne'er did I see such teeny, tiny stitches;
    Ne'er did I see
    Stitches so wee!

This picture of Paris shows the quaint
manner of selling books on the walls along
the river Seine. In the background is the
Cathedral of Notre Dame de Paris.

At Paris There's a Fountain

At Paris there's a bright,
There's a bright sparkling fountain.
    O drip, O drop! O drip, O drop!
      Drip, fountain, drop!

And thither came to bathe,
Who but three pretty maidens.
O drip, O drop! O drip, O drop!
      Drip, fountain, drop!

Just then passed by that way,
Little small King of England.
    O drip, O drop! O drip, O drop!
      Drip, fountain, drop!

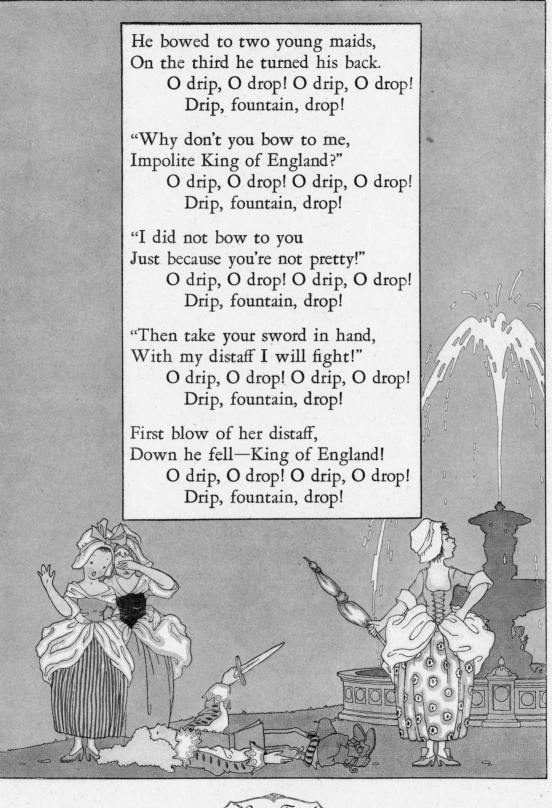

He bowed to two young maids,
On the third he turned his back.
    O drip, O drop! O drip, O drop!
    Drip, fountain, drop!

"Why don't you bow to me,
Impolite King of England?"
    O drip, O drop! O drip, O drop!
    Drip, fountain, drop!

"I did not bow to you
Just because you're not pretty!"
    O drip, O drop! O drip, O drop!
    Drip, fountain, drop!

"Then take your sword in hand,
With my distaff I will fight!"
    O drip, O drop! O drip, O drop!
    Drip, fountain, drop!

First blow of her distaff,
Down he fell—King of England!
    O drip, O drop! O drip, O drop!
    Drip, fountain, drop!

At Paris Near the Little Bridge

At Paris near the little bridge,
By a fountain, fon-fon-tain-o,
My father built a house,—ron, ron!
Ton-ton, ton-ton, ton-tain-o!
Now, good day, my pretty Margoton,
Spring brings you back again-o!

The carpenters who worked thereon,
By the fountain, fon-fon-tain-o,
Asked me to tell my name,—ron, ron!
Ton-ton, ton-ton, ton-tain-o!
Now, good day, my pretty Margoton,
Spring brings you back again-o!

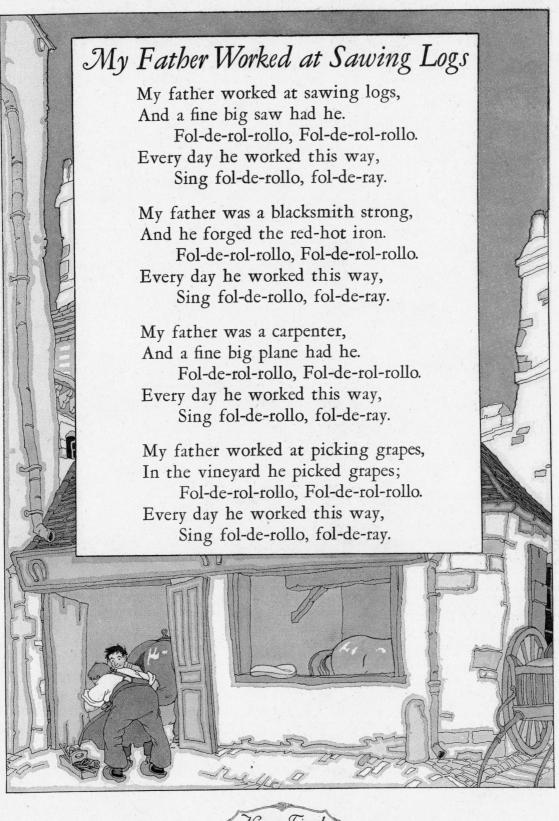

My Father Worked at Sawing Logs

My father worked at sawing logs,
And a fine big saw had he.
　　Fol-de-rol-rollo, Fol-de-rol-rollo.
Every day he worked this way,
　　Sing fol-de-rollo, fol-de-ray.

My father was a blacksmith strong,
And he forged the red-hot iron.
　　Fol-de-rol-rollo, Fol-de-rol-rollo.
Every day he worked this way,
　　Sing fol-de-rollo, fol-de-ray.

My father was a carpenter,
And a fine big plane had he.
　　Fol-de-rol-rollo, Fol-de-rol-rollo.
Every day he worked this way,
　　Sing fol-de-rollo, fol-de-ray.

My father worked at picking grapes,
In the vineyard he picked grapes;
　　Fol-de-rol-rollo, Fol-de-rol-rollo.
Every day he worked this way,
　　Sing fol-de-rollo, fol-de-ray.

Girofle, Girofla

You have such pretty daughters,—
    Giroflay, Giroflah!
You have such pretty daughters;—
    I'm in love,—ah, ah!
O, they are fair and lovely,—
    Giroflay, Giroflah!
Pray give to me one only,—
    I'm in love,—ah, ah!

No hair of one I'll give you,—
    Giroflay, Giroflah!
I'll seek the woods then lonely!
    I'm in love,—ah, ah!
And what will you do there, pray,—
    Giroflay, Giroflah!
The violets I'll gather,—
    I'm in love,—ah, ah!

Nursery Friends
from France

And if the King should meet you,
  Giroflay, Giroflah?
I'll make him three fine curtsies,
  I'm in love,—ah, ah!
And if the Queen should meet you,
  Giroflay, Giroflah?
I'll make her six fine curtsies,
  I'm in love,—ah, ah!

Allegro

Que t'as de bel - les fil - les Gi - ro - flé, Gi - ro - fla! Que
You have such pret - ty daugh - ters Gi - ro - flay Gi - ro - flah! You

t'as de bel - les fil - les, L'amour m'y comp - t'ra Ell's sont bell's et gen - til - les, Gi - ro -
have such pret - ty daugh - ters I'm in love, ah, ah! Oh, they are fair and love - ly, Gi - ro -

flé, Gi - ro - fla! Ell's sont bell's et gen - til - les, L'amour m'y comp - t'ra.
flay, Gi - ro - flah! Pray give to me one on - ly, I'm in love, ah, ah!

By the Tail, Ail, Ail

By the tail, ail, ail,
By the tail, by the tail!
By the tail, ail, ail,
By the tail, bang, bang!

Vivace.

A la queue leu! leu! A la queue, à la queue, A la queue leu leu, A la queue Ouin Ouin!

Little Hen Upon the Wall

Little hen upon the wall,
There you peck for wheat grains small;
    Pick, pick, peck;
    Pick, peck, pay!
Flop your tail and fly away!

Little cock below the wall,
There you peck for wheat grains small;
    Pick, pick, peck;
    Pick, peck, pay!
Lift your leg and strut away!

An Old Round from Rouen

'Twas the cock of the Madeleine,
Who fought last week with might and main,
'Gainst the cock of Saint Maclou.
Such a fuss they made, those two,
Men threw sticks at each one's back,—
Whack, whack!

Rouen, the ancient capital of Normandy, is a most picturesque old city on the river Seine, set in a semicircle of beautiful green hills. It has narrow, crooked, little streets, with quaint old houses of plaster and timber, jutting out every which way. Over all, rise the tall, graceful spires of its many churches, carved delicately out of stone. It was in Rouen that Joan of Arc, the French girl who once saved France, was so long imprisoned by the English.

'Twas Dames of Rouen

Twas ladies of Rou-on, they say,—
Who made a pie so huge one day,
The city gates 'twould not go through,
They had to cut it quite in two!
Inside they found a duck, good lack!
He started off to sing, quack! quack!
Said he: "All men are rogues, I swear,
Long live Rou-on's fine ladies fair!

Nursery Friends
from France

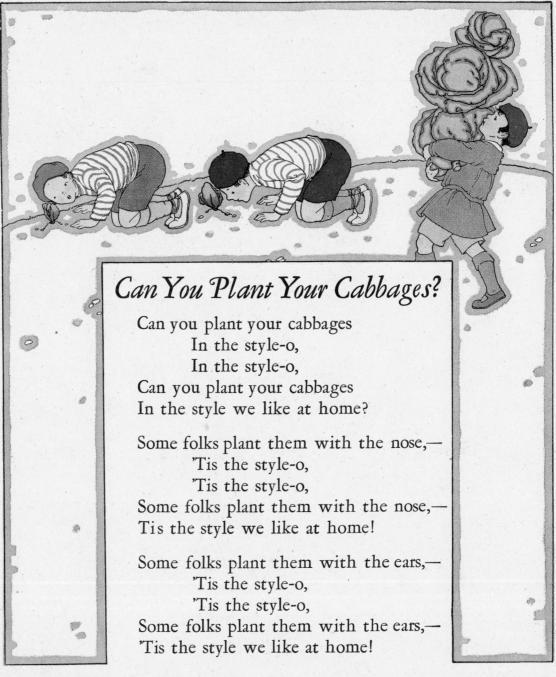

Can You Plant Your Cabbages?

Can you plant your cabbages
  In the style-o,
  In the style-o,
Can you plant your cabbages
In the style we like at home?

Some folks plant them with the nose,—
  'Tis the style-o,
  'Tis the style-o,
Some folks plant them with the nose,—
Tis the style we like at home!

Some folks plant them with the ears,—
  'Tis the style-o,
  'Tis the style-o,
Some folks plant them with the ears,—
'Tis the style we like at home!

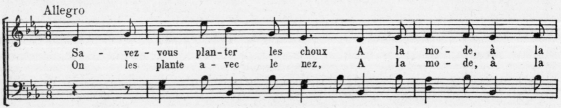

Allegro

Sa - vez - vous plan-ter les choux A la mo - de, à la
On les plante a - vec le nez, A la mo - de, à la

Some folks plant them with the heels,—
   'Tis the style-o,
   'Tis the style-o,
Some folks plant them with heels,—
'Tis the style we like at home!

Some folks plant them with the chin,—
   'Tis the style-o,
   'Tis the style-o,
Some folks plant them with the chin,—
Tis the style we like at home!

Some folks plant them with the thumb,—
   'Tis the style-o,
   'Tis the style-o,
Some folks plant them with the thumb,—
'Tis the style we like at home!

mo - de, Sa - vez-vous plan-ter les choux, A la mo - de de chez nous?
mo - de, On les plante a - vec le nez, A la mo - de de chez nous?

It Rains! It Rains, My Lassie!

It rains! It rains, my lassie!
Hurry thy snow-white sheep!
Come into our cottage;
Quick, now! Climb the steep!
Hark! amid the tree-tops,
Noisy rain-drops crash.
The storm, the storm's upon us!
See,—the lightning flash!

Nursery Friends
from France

114

And hearest thou the thunder,
Rolling as it comes?
By my side take shelter,—
Lo! It rolls like drums!
Ah, but there's our cottage,
There's my mother,—see!
And sister Anne who opens
Wide the shed for thee!

Good evening, O my mother!
Sister Anne, a light!
A shepherdess I'm bringing
Home to you tonight!
We'll take care, my mother,
Of her pretty sheep,
And with fresh straw in plenty,
Her little lamb we'll keep.

Outside the wind is whistling,
'Gainst yonder cliff and byre.
Pray take this chair for supper,
And sit thee by the fire!
Here's bread and cheese before thee,
But,—thou dost not eat,—
Thou thinkest of the storm, then—
Did it tire thy feet?

Ah, well, here by my mother,
In our home, we pray,
Sweet shepherdess, just rest thee,
Till the break of day.
Good night now, my lassie;
When the day shall come,
I'll take thy hand and lead thee
Safely to thy home.

Allegretto

Il pleut, il pleut, ber-gè-re, Presse tes blancs moutons; Al-lons sous la chau-
It rains, it rains, my las-sie, Hur-ry thy snow-white sheep: Come in-to our

miè-re, Ber-gè-re, vite al-lons!___ J'en-tends sous le feuil-la-ge
cot-tage Quick now climb the steep!___ Hark! a-mid the tree-tops

L'eau qui tombe à grand bruit; Voi-ci, voi-ci l'o-ra-ge, Voi-ci l'é-clair qui luit!
Nois-y rain-drops crash; The storm, the storm's up-on us; See, the lightning flash!

The Beggar's Song

I go my way,
And have no cares all day!
I go my way;
I go my way!

I've nothing at all for clothing,
Save a single shirt, you see;
The raindrops do my washing;
Fine weather dries for me!

My house is a hollow tree-trunk,
With that I'm quite content;
In such a house as that is,
I'm never asked for rent!

The father of my grandfather
The king of beggars was he;
And I, in my rags and tatters,
Am happy as can be!

I go my way,
And have no cares all day;
I go my way;
I go my way!

In Paris there Lived a Lady

In Paris there lived a lady,
    Lovely as the day was she;
But she had a proud maid-servant,
Who wished, who wished, who wished to be
    Still more fair, more fair than she,
        And could not be!

Off the maid went to the druggist;
    "I want face-paint,—red" cried she.
"'Tis six francs the ounce, my pretty;
That's two, that's two, two crowns!" said he.
    "Give me then a half an ounce, sir,—
        Here's a crown, you see!"

"When your face you start a-painting,
    Do it in the dark," he said.
"First you must put out your candle,
Then daub, then daub, then daub the red!
    After that you'll be as pretty
        As you should!" he said.

In the night she did her painting,
    Decked herself at break of day
In hose of silk, and fine green skirt,
And white, and white, white bodice gay!
    Forth then, strutting, to the city
        She took her way!

This picture was suggested by the famous portrait of Madame Recamier (1777-1845) by Jacques Louis David. It was at the home of the beautiful Madame Recamier that the greatest literary and political leaders gathered in the days of Napoleon and later.

Nursery Friends from France

As she went in proud parading,
    Lo! she met a gay young beau;
Lack! where do you go, Manetta,
All daubed, all daubed, all daubed up so?
    Face as black as any coal-man's!
      Hah, hah! Ho, ho!

Woe is me! she seeks the druggist.
    "'Twas no paint you sold!" she said.
"Nay, I gave you my best blacking;—
'Twas for, 'twas for, for shoes instead!
    Wanting to outshine your mistress
      Was wrong!" he said.

Nursery Friends
from France

The Clock

Ding dong! I am the clock!
The castle clock am I!
Ding dong! Ding dong! Tick tock!
Up in the tower so high!

From height of thy tall tower,
Thy bell, O clock, now ring,
And tell us, pray, the hour
With thy Ding dong! Ding! Ding!

Hens to Sell

I have hens to sell you!
Red or white, I tell you!
Four sous here,
Four sous here,—
Mary, Mary, turn, my dear!

J'ai des poul's à - ven-dre Des roug's et des blan-ches A quat' sous à quat' sous Ma-rie, Ma-rie, tour-nez vous.

La Verdi, La Verdon

Ah, if I had a sou so round,
I'd buy the best sheep to be found.
    La Verdi, La Verdon,
And hoop la! Skip you now, La Verdon!

I'd shear him when the time came round,
And celebrate with merry sound.
    La Verdi, La Verdon,
And hoop la! Skip you now, La Verdon!

But ah! three rogues come sneaking 'round,
They'll steal my fleece from off the ground.
    La Verdi, La Verdon,
And hoop la! Skip you now, La Verdon!

I'll chase to Lyons, I'll be bound;
Give back that fleece now, pound for pound.
    La Verdi, La Verdon,
And hoop la! Skip you now, La Verdon!

Rose of Damascus

Away back home at father's,
    O shepherd lad;
  The orange trees do grow,—
With a ho! la-derry-ro!
  The orange trees do grow,—
Rose of Damascus, Oh! heigho!

The branches are full laden,
    O shepherd lad;
  They're drooping down so low,—
With a ho! la-derry-ro!
  They're drooping down so low,—
Rose of Damascus, Oh! heigho!

I say then to my father,
    O shepherd lad;
  "A-picking now let's go,—
With a ho! la-derry-ro!
  A-picking now let's go,"—
Rose of Damascus, Oh! heigho!

And then I take a ladder,
    O shepherd lad;
  A basket take also,—
With a ho! la-derry-ro!
  A basket take also,—
Rose of Damascus, Oh! heigho!

The yellowest I gather,
    O shepherd lad,
  And leave the rest to grow,—
With a ho! la-derry-ro!
  And leave the rest to grow,—
Rose of Damascus, Oh! heigho!

From Fair Auvergne Returning

From fair Auvergne returning,
Auvergne, my own countree,
I journeyed down the highway,
The highway to Paree;—
I sang Savoy's sweet chants,
I danced the mountain dance!
Hay, gay, jog, jog!
Hay, gay, jog, jog!
Now come and see the dance of
The little ground-hog!
Now come and see the dance of
The little ground-hog!
The little ground-hog!
The little ground-hog!

I met a dame quite toothless:
"Ho! little boy," said she,
"Come, let me see you dancing
The dance of your countree!
O, sing Savoy's sweet chants,
O, dance the mountain dance!"
Hay, gay, jog, jog!
Hay, gay, jog, jog!
You shall not see the dance of
    The little ground-hog!
You shall not see the dance of
    The little ground-hog!
        The little ground-nog!
          The little ground-hog!

I met a pretty lassie:
"My fine young man," said she,
"Pray show me how you're dancing
The dance of your countree!
Pray sing Savoy's sweet chants,
Pray dance the mountain dance!"
Hay, gay, jog, jog!
Hay, gay, jog, jog!
I showed the lass the dance of
    The little ground-hog!
I showed the lass the dance of
    The little ground-hog!
        The little ground-hog!
          The little ground-hog!

Auvergne is a province of central France. Upper Auvergne is rugged and mountainous, and many a sturdy mountaineer leaves his poor home there to seek his fortunes in Paris. In these mountains lives the little, chubby, short-legged, busy-tailed marmot, woodchuck or groundhog, who dances so gaily through this song. The men of Auvergne are related to other sturdy mountaineers, the men of Savoy. Savoy is a province to eastward, bordering on Italy, Switzerland and the beautiful Lake of Geneva. Savoy has many, many mountains, among which, most beautiful of all, towers up the glistening, snow-capped peak of Mont Blanc.

Con moto

En revenant d'Au-ver-gne, En revenant d'Au-verg-ne, En revenant d'Au-ver-gne, d'Au-
From fair Auvergne return - ing, From fair Auvergne returning, From fair Auvergne return - ing, Au-

verg-ne, mon pa-ys. Passant par la Li-ma-gne, Passant par la Li-ma-gne, Passant par la Li-
vergne my own countree. I journey'd down the highway I journey'd down the highway, I journey'd down the

ma-gne, D'la Limagne à Paris; Chantant la Savoy-ar - de, Dansant la Monta-gnar-de: Eh
highway, the highway to Pa - ree; I sang Savoy's sweet chants, I danced the mountain dance Hay

gai Coco, Eh gai Coco! Eh, venez voir la dan - se Du pe-tit mar-mot Eh venez voir la
gay, jog jog, Hay gay, jog jog! Now come and see the dance of the lit-tle ground-hog, Now come and see the

dan-se Du pe-tit marmot,_____ Du pe-tit marmot _____ Du pe tit mar-mot
dance of the little ground-hog. The lit-tle ground-hog, The lit-tle ground - hog.

To the Woods Let Us Go

To the woods, let us go,
While old Wolf's not there, O ho!
He will catch, catch us, catch,
If he's there, you know!

Wolf, are you there?
  No, I'm putting on my coat!

To the woods, let us go,
While old Wolf's not there, O ho!

  I am Wolf! I am Wolf!
    And I'll catch you,—see!
I am Deer! I am Deer!
No, you'll not catch me!

To the woods, let us go,
While old Wolf's not there, O ho!
He will catch, catch us, catch,
If he's there, you know!

Wolf, are you there?
  No, I'm putting on my boots!

To the woods, let us go,
While old Wolf's not there, O ho!

I am Wolf! I am Wolf!
And I'll catch you,—see!
I am Deer! I am Deer!
No, you'll not catch me!

To the woods, let us go,
While old Wolf's not there, O ho!
He will catch, catch us, catch,
If he's there, you know!

Wolf, are you there?
Yes, I'm taking down my gun!

Then we'll run away!

When French children play this game, one hides himself and pretends to be the Wolf. The others form in a line and march around, following the leader, who plays he is the Deer. When the Wolf springs out of his hiding place, he tries to catch and carry back to his den the child who is at the end of the line, following the Deer. The child resists, but the Wolf always ends by carrying him off. In this way he takes all the children in the line until there are no more. Then the game is ended.

Allegretto moderato.
CHORUS.

Prom'nons-nous dans les bois Tan - dis que le loup n'y est pas; Si le loup y é-
To the woods let us go While old Wolf's not there, O ho! He would catch, catch us,

Speak. CHORUS. WOLF. *f* CHORUS.

tait Il nous man - ge - rait. *"Loup y es-tu?"* *"Non, je mets mon habit."* *Prom'nons-nous dans les*
catch If he could, you know. "Wolf, are you there?" "No, I'm putting on my coat." To the woods let us

THE WOLF.

bois, Tan - dis que le loup n'y est pas. *Je suis loup, je suis loup qui te*
go While old Wolf's not there, O ho! I am Wolf, I am Wolf and I'll

THE DEER.

man - ge - ra. *Je suis biche, je suis biche qui me dé - fen - dra.*
catch you, see? I am Deer, I am Deer, No, you'll not catch me.

Eho! Eho! Eho!

Eho! Eho! Eho!
To the fields go the sheep!
Eho! Eho! Eho!
In the woods, wolves, I trow;
While by bright fountains deep,
Or where fresh brooklets flow,
Little lambs wash and leap.
O'er the green, there they go!

Allegretto

Eho! Eho! Eho!
Eho! Eho! Eho!

Les agneaux vont aux plai - nes
To the fields go the sheep

Eho! Eho! Eho!
Eho! Eho! Eho!

Et les loups sont aux bois
In the woods, wolves I trow

Tan' qu'au bord des fontai - nes
While by bright fountains deep

Ou dans les frai ruis
Or where fresh brook-lets

seaux
flow,

Les moutons baign'leurs lai - nes,
Lit - tle lambs wash and leap,

Y, dansants au pré au.
O'er the green, there they go.

Nursery Friends
from France

This picture was suggested by a painting called "Shepherds
and Shepherdesses" by François Boucher (1703-1770).
Boucher, with Jean Antoine Watteau (1684-1721) his
master, covered the walls and ceilings of French palaces
with the most fanciful figures of shepherds and shepherdesses, dressed in garments no shepherd could ever have worn,
and enjoying all the delights of the countryside without
toil or labor. Their shepherds were not laborers but aristo-
crats masquerading and playing at being shepherds.

In the Vineyard

"Come, sweetheart, to the vineyard;
Tis rich beyond compare!"

"I won't go in the vineyard
When there is nothing there!
'Tis only thorns are growing;
Of thorns I would beware!"

"Come, come, my pretty, enter;
I'll give you gloves to wear!"

I've a Bouquet

I've a bouquet here at my side,
To whom shall I give it, pray?
    To mad'moiselle,
    Over here, over there!
Ah, who shall have it, I say?
    Ma'mselle, skip away!
    Ma'mselle, dance away!
Kiss the one you love best,—hooray!
Hark! I hear the drum that beats,
And mother calling to me,—
Quick now! Quick now! Hurry up,
And kiss the fairest maid you see!

Song of the Oats

Shall I tell you how, how, how
    The farmer sows his oats?
My father sows them just this way,
And rests from work at noon each day.
    Clap your feet!
    Clap your hands, too!
Swing round the maid who's nearest you!
O grain! O grain! O grain, grain, grain,
Fine weather brings you back again!

Shall I tell you how, how, how
    The farmer cuts his oats?
My father cuts them just this way,
And rests from work at noon each day.
    Clap your feet!
    Clap your hands, too!
Swing round the maid who's nearest you!
O grain! O grain! O grain, grain, grain,
Fine weather brings you back again!

In France red poppies, white daisies and blue cornflowers grow in amongst the grain as in this picture, decorating the fields with brilliant patches of the national colors of France.

Nursery Friends from France

The Lass at Haying Harvest

Never will I forget
The lass at the haying harvest;
Never forget my sweet
At the harvest of the wheat.
Rich men would not give their daughters,
Though for them I should entreat.
Never will I forget
The lass at the haying harvest;
Never forget my sweet
At the harvest of the wheat.

These laborers are not the fanciful mas-
queraders of a Watteau or a Boucher, but
real French peasant figures as painted by
Jean François Millet (1814-1875) or Jules
Breton (1827-1906) who, in direct con-
trast to Watteau and Boucher, wished to
show toil as it really is, with all its
simple dignity.

A Song to the Oxen

Come on, my pretty pair:
    Come on, come on,—so!
We must do our work with care;
    Come on, come on,—so!

Make straight your furrows now:
    Come on, come on,—so!
Come, my little children, plough!
    Come on, come on,—so!

Come on, my pretty pair:
    Come on, come on,—so!
My two little brothers,—on;
    Come on, come on,—so!

This picture was suggested by a painting
by Rosa Bonheur (1822-1899) the great
French painter of animals.

Nursery Friends
from France

The Poor Laborer

The poor laborer
Is content all the day,
When he follows the plough,
He sings alway;
For there's no King nor Prince,
No Duke, nor Seigneur,
But lives from the work
Of the poor laborer!

The Shepherdess

There was a shepherd lassie,
O ron, ron, ron! Pitty pat-upon.
There was a shepherd lassie,
Who watched her sheep just yon,
ron, ron,
Who watched her sheep just yon!

She made a cheese, that lassie,
O ron, ron, ron! Pitty pat-upon!
She made a cheese, that lassie,
From milk of sheep, ton, ton,
ron, ron,
From milk of sheep, ton, ton.

Her cat stood by a-watching,
O ron, ron, ron! Pitty pat-upon!
Her cat stood by a-watching,
With roguish air looked on,
ron, ron,
With roguish air looked on.

Don't put your paw in, pussy,
O ron, ron, ron! Pitty pat-upon!
Don't put your paw in, pussy,
Or you'll be switched, ton, ton,
ron, ron,
Or you'll be switched, ton, ton.

He did not put his paw in,
O ron, ron, ron! Pitty pat-upon!
He did not put his paw in,—
Put in his chin, chin, chon,
ron, ron,
Put in his chin, chin, chon!

Allegretto

Il é - tait un' ber - gè - re, Et ron ron ron, Pe - tit
El - le fit un fro - ma - ge, Et ron ron ron, Pe - tit

pa - ta - pon, Il é - tait un' ber - gè - re Qui gar - dait ses mou-
pa - ta - pon, El - le fit un fro - ma - ge Du lait de ses mou-

tons, ron ron, Qui gar - dait ses mou - tons.
tons, ron ron, Du lait de ses mou - tons.

He Runs, He Runs, Ferret Runs

In playing this game the French children form a circle. They are given a rope which has been passed through a small ring and tied together at the ends. All put their hands on this circle of rope, and, as they sing, they keep their hands moving, secretly passing the ring from one child to another. In the center of the circle stands a child who is trying to guess which hand is over the ring. When he guesses correctly and touches the hand, the game stops; the child who held the ring becomes "it" and goes into the center of the circle. The other child takes his place and the game goes on.

Allegro.

Il court, il court, le fu-ret, Le fu-ret du bois, més-dam's; Il court, il court, le fu-
He runs, he runs; fer-ret runs, Fer-ret of the woods, my la-dies. Runs, he runs; fer-ret

ret, Le fu-ret du bois jo-li. Il a pas-sé par i-ci; Le fu-ret du bois més-
runs, Pret-ty fer-ret of the woods. He has just run past us here, Fer-ret of the woods, my

He runs, he runs, ferret runs,
  Ferret of the woods, my ladies.
Runs, he runs, ferret runs,
  Pretty ferret of the woods.
He has just run past us here,
  Ferret of the woods, my ladies.
He has just run past us here,
  Pretty ferret of the wood
He runs, he runs, ferret runs,
  Ferret of the woods, my ladies!
Runs, he runs, ferret runs,
  Pretty ferret of the woods!

dam-es, Il a pas-sé par i-ci, Le fu-ret du bois jo-li. Il court, il court, le fu-
la-dies. He has just run past us here, Pret-ty fer-ret of the woods. He runs, he runs, fer-ret

ret, Le fu-ret du bois més-dam's; Il court, il court, le ju-ret, Le fu-ret du bois jo-li.
runs, Fer-ret of the woods, my la-dies. Runs, he runs; fer-ret runs, Pret-ty fer-ret of the woods.

Where Are You Going?

Good day, Madame!
Good day, Madame!
Where are you going, Madame?
To the House in the Woods!
You to the House in the Woods, I to the House in the Woods;
Let us then go in company.

Have you a husband?
Yes!
What is his name, your husband?
Big John!
Your husband, Big John, my husband, Big John;
You to the House in the Woods, I to the House in the Woods;
Let us then go in company.

Have you a baby?
Yes!
What is his name, your baby?
Niniche!
Your baby, Niniche, my baby, Niniche;
Your husband, Big John, my husband, Big John;
You to the House in the Woods, I to the House in the Woods;
Let us then go in company.

Nursery Friends from France

Have you a cradle?
Yes!
What is its name, your cradle?
Baby-bye!
Your cradle, Baby-bye, my cradle, Baby-bye;
Your baby, Niniche, my baby, Niniche;
Your husband, Big John, my husband, Big John;
You to the House in the Woods, I to the House in the Woods;
Let us then go in company.

Have you a servant?
Yes!
What is his name, your servant?
Not-too-bad!
Your servant, Not-too-bad, my servant, Not-too-bad;
Your cradle, Baby-bye, my cradle, Baby-bye;
Your baby, Niniche, my baby, Niniche;
Your husband, Big John, my husband, Big John;
You to the House in the Woods, I to the House in the Woods;
Let us then go in company.

'Twas a Lawyer

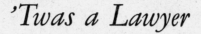

'Twas a lawyer over yon,—
    Tour, tour, tour-la-ri-retta!
To a wedding is he gone,—
    Tour-la-ri-retta; lir-ron-fon!

Went into an inn anon,—
    Tour, tour, tour-la-ri-retta:
Eggs to fry! Pray put them on,—
    Tour-la-ri-retta; lir-ron-fon!

When with supper he was done,—
    Tour, tour, tour-la-ri-retta!
To his bed he would be gone,—
    Tour-la-ri-retta; lir-ron-fon!

Bed of straw he lay upon,—
    Tour, tour, tour-la-ri-retta!
All night long he snored,—flon, flon!
    Tour-la-ri-retta! lin-ron-fon!

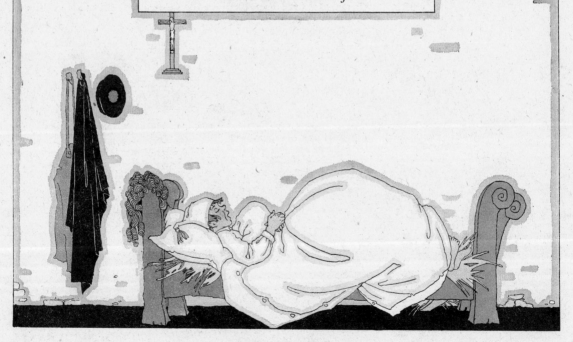

Nursery Friends
from France

The Baker's Dame

The baker's dame has bags of gold,
    O money to burn has she;
Yes she has,—I did behold!
I saw the baker's dame at her gold;—
    With mine own eyes I did see!

My Father had a Garden Gay

My father had a garden gay;
My brother watered it each day.
 Piberli, piberlo,
 Pin d'or derino!

My sister picked the pinks that grew,—
Heavens, suppose my father knew!
 Piberli, piberlo,
 Pin d'or derino!

My father loved those pinks so well,—
But then there's no one who will tell!
 Piberli, piberlo,
 Pin d'or derino!

The birds will tell within the wood.
They'll not speak, they never could.
 Piberli, piberlo,
 Pin d'or derino!

Ah, yes they can! They speak,—'tis so,
They'll tell your secret if they know!
 Piberli, piberlo,
 Pin d'or derino!

What will they, in their latin, say?
Leave the flowers in the garden, pray
 Piberli, piberlo,
 Pin d'or derino!

Nursery Friends from France

Song of the Flowers

You, O my Rose, my pretty thing,
Come, if you please, inside this ring.
All of your charms now proudly show,
Making so fair our garden row.
      Come once more, come, come, we sing,
        Flowers of the lovely spring!

You, Mister Coxcomb, you I know,
Who play so well the courtly beau.
Now, keeping time, salute Miss Rose,
She'll make a curtsy, I suppose!
      Come once more, come, come, we sing,
        Flowers of the lovely Spring!

You, too, my modest flower and fair,
Men sing your frank face everywhere,
You, little Violet, my friend,
Your perfumes to the fields now send.
      Come once more, come, come, we sing,
        Flowers of the lovely Spring!

And Mister Dahlia, you so gay,
All in your clothes of holiday,
Sir Dahlia to our dance we call,—
The door will open wide for all.
      Come once more, come, come, we sing
        Flowers of the lovely Spring.

I Planted a Rosebush

I planted a rosebush,
My Mignon, in your bower;
At ev'ning set it out;
    By morning, ah!
    Tra la, tra la!
By morning 'twas in flower!

I said to it, "Rosebush,
You've bloomed before the hour;
Ah, why did you not wait
    For April, ah!
    Tra la, tra la,
For April's pretty shower?

"Ah, why did you not wait
For April's pretty shower,
When earth is all abud,
    And greenwoods, ah!
    Tra la, tra la!
And greenwoods all in flower?"

The Gardener Boy

I got up one fine morning
The sunshine to enjoy;
But as I walked, I met,
      Ho, ho!
The daughter of a carpenter,—
I, the gardener boy!

Where do you go so early,
My pretty one and coy?
I'm going to the church,
      Ho, ho!
Now hear the bells a-ringing,—
You, the gardener boy!

For church it is too early;
My garden you'll enjoy;
I take her little hand,
      Ho, ho!
And lead her to the garden,—
I, the gardener boy!

Rondel

Old Time has lost his mantle drear,
    Of wind, of winter, and of rain.
    He's clothed in broidery again
Of radiant sunlight bright and clear;
And ne'er a beast or bird I hear
    But in his joy sings this refrain:
"Old Time has lost his mantle drear,
    Of wind, of winter, and of rain."
Now fountain, river, brook and mere,
    Their finest robes once more regain,
    Bespangled like some goldsmith's chain.
Aye, each, new clothed, doth now appear.
Old Time has lost his mantle drear,
    Of wind, of winter, and of rain.

Charles d'Orleans (1391-1464)

This picture was suggested by an ancient French tapestry showing a hunting scene of the period of Charles d'Orleans.

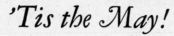

'Tis the May!

Trimousette, 'tis the May, month of May,
'Tis the pretty month of May!

Coming from the fields at noon,
There we saw the wheat stalks plume,
Saw the hawthorne all in bloom
Before God.

Trimousette, 'tis the May, month of May,
'Tis the pretty month of May!

These figures were suggested by a painting called "Summer" by Nicholas Lancret, a painter of the same fanciful French type as Watteau and Boucher.

Nursery Friends from France

The Sun

Lovely sun, in the skies;—
Shine all rosy when you rise!
Lovely sun, in the skies;—
Shine to bid us ope our eyes!

In the East when you appear,
All is fresh and smiling here,
And the dewy earth, behold!
Sparkling 'neath your rays of gold!

Lovely sun, in the skies;—
Shine all rosy when you rise!
Lovely sun, in the skies;—
Shine to bid us ope our eyes!

When the sky is bright in Spring,
Then thy rays, all shimmering,
Bring us back the flowers to bloom,
Gayest colors, sweet perfume!

Lovely sun, in the skies;—
Shine all rosy when you rise!
Lovely sun, in the skies;—
Shine to bid us ope our eyes!

The Laurels of the Wood

We'll seek no more the woods; we're cutting laurels today;
My pretty lassie there, wilt dance with me, I pray?
        Come into the dance now!
        See how we dance now!
        Skip now! Dance now!
        Swing whatever lass you may!

The laurels of the wood, they must not wither, nay!
Each one in turn shall go and gather in a spray.
        Come into the dance now!
        See how we dance now!
        Skip now! Dance now!
        Swing whatever lass you may!

If Grassyhopper sleeps, oh, do not hurt him, pray!
The nightingale's sweet song shall wake him to the day.
>Come into the dance now!
>See how we dance now!
>Skip now! Dance now!
>Swing whatever lass you may!

And Jeanne, the shepherdess, will come with basket so gay,
To gather berries there, and flowers of the May.
>Come into the dance now!
>See how we dance now!
>Skip now! Dance now!
>Swing whatever lass you may!

O Grassyhopper mine, wake up and sing away,
The laurels of the wood are blossoming today!
>Come into the dance now!
>See how we dance now!
>Skip now! Dance now!
>Swing whatever lass you may!

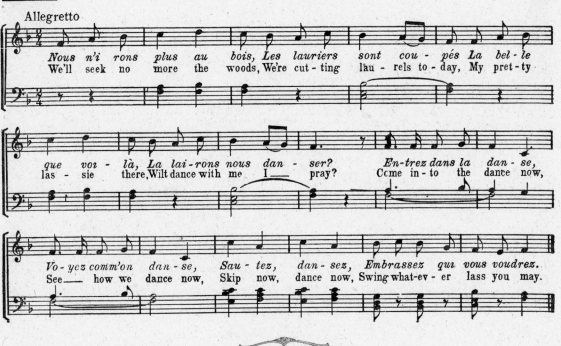

Allegretto

Nous n'i rons plus au bois, Les lauriers sont cou - pés La bel - le
We'll seek no more the woods, We're cut - ting lau - rels to - day, My pret - ty

que voi - là, La lai - rons nous dan - ser? En-trez dans la dan - se,
las - sie there, Wilt dance with me I pray? Come in - to the dance now,

Vo - yez comm'on dan - se, Sau - tez, dan - sez, Embrassez qui vous voudrez.
See how we dance now, Skip now, dance now, Swing what-ev - er lass you may.

The Two Heroes

Two rabbits once swore, "We'll be heroes bold,
We're worth a hundred zouaves, we hold!"

They vowed to strike a mighty blow,
And to make an end of old Wolf, their foe.

Each swore to his wife to bring to her,
As a little gift, old Wolf's gray fur.

Each promised his son Wolf's tail, mayhap,
To wear as a feather in his cap.

Drums beat as they marched and never ceased,
Till they reached the lair of the huge old beast.

Just then he appeared, old Wolf so hale,
They saw indeed,—saw the tip of his tail!

Then the two heroes fled as one hare from the place;
And each one brought back—a scratched-up face!

Nursery Friends
from France

I Went to Bagnolet

I went to Bagnolet to school,
And there I met a huge old mule
    A-planting, planting carrots!
My Madeleine, I love you so,
    I'm talking foolishness, I know!

A little further on I saw
A jaunty little man of straw
    A-dancing a gavotte!
My Madeleine, I love you so,
    I'm talking foolishness, I know!

Bagnolet (Bon yo lay´) is a town near Paris.

Nursery Friends from France

From Versailles
I was Returning

From Versailles I was returning,
Passing by St. Cloud, click, clack!
When I met a little mannie
With his wife upon his back.
I've enough of my wife, sir,—
Buy her now, good lack!

Versailles is a town near Paris, famous for the great palace with beautiful gardens and fountains, built there by Louis XIV in 1661. St. Cloud is also near Paris, and once had a royal chateau.

I am taking her to sell her,
And I offer her to you.
She cost a thousand dollars,
But I'll sell her for a sou.
I've enough of my wife, sir.
Buy her now, pray do!

Comrades of the Marjolaine

Who goes there so late, I say,
Comrades of the Marjolaine?
Who goes there so late, I say,
Gay, gay, over the way?

Allegretto

Qu'est- c'qui passe i - ci si tard, Com - pa - gnons de la Mar - jo -
C'est le chev - a - lier du guet, Com - pa - gnons de la Mar - jo -
Who goes there so late, I say, Com - rades of the Mar - jo -

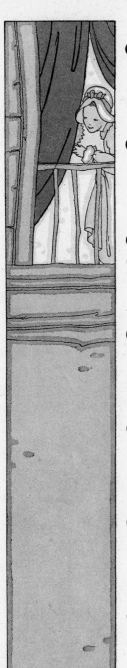

'Tis the night watch, bold and gay,
Comrades of the Marjolaine.
　'Tis the night watch, bold and gay,
　　Gay, gay, over the way.

What's your wish, Sir?　Tell me, pray,
Comrades of the Marjolaine?
　What's your wish, Sir?　Tell me, pray,
　　Gay, gay, over the way?

I would wed tomorrow day,
Comrades of the Marjolaine;
　I would wed tomorrow day,
　　Gay, gay, over the way.

I've no maids to give you, nay,
Comrades of the Marjolaine.
　I've no maids to give you, nay,
　　Gay, gay, over the way.

But you've daughters, people say,
Comrades of the Marjolaine.
　But you've daughters, people say,
　　Gay, gay, over the way.

They're in bed, so do not stay,
Comrades of the Marjolaine.
　They're in bed, so do not stay,
　　Gay, gay, over the way.

One's awake,—you can't gainsay.
Comrades of the Marjolaine.
　One's awake,—you can't gainsay,
　　Gay, gay, over the way.

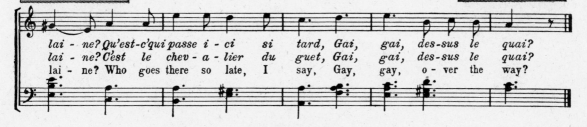

lai - ne? Qu'est-c'qui passe i - ci　si　tard, Gai,　gai, des-sus le　quai?
lai - ne? C'est　le　chev - a - lier　du　guet, Gai,　gai, des-sus le　quai?
lai - ne? Who　goes there so　late, I　say, Gay,　gay,　o - ver the　way?

What wouldst give my daughters, pray,
Comrades of the Marjolaine?
What wouldst give my daughters, pray,
Gay, gay, over the way?

Gold and gems in fine array,
Comrades of the Marjolaine;
Gold and gems in fine array,
Gay, gay, over the way.

They've no liking for display,
Comrades of the Marjolaine;
They've no liking for display,
Gay, gay, over the way.

But my heart I'll give away,
Comrades of the Marjolaine;
But my heart I'll give away,
Gay, gay, over the way.

Choose one then without delay,
Comrades of the Marjolaine;
Choose one then without delay,
Gay, gay, over the way.

My Father Built Me
a Chateau

My father built me a chateau,
'Twas small but pretty, you must know.
He built it of three bricks, I trow,—
The bricks were silver, shining so!
Inside, there was a fountain fair,—
Threewhite ducks went swimming there!

Ah, My Fine Chateau!

This is a game the French children play. They form two groups, and begin to dance in two rings, singing and holding hands. As long as the second group refuses the objects offered by the first group, the game continues. When the second group accepts, the game ends.

First Circle Sings:

Ah, my fine chateau,
 Aunty, tira, lira, lira,
Ah, my fine chateau,
 Aunty, tira, lira, lo!

Second Circle Sings:

We will break it down,
 Aunty, tira, lira, lira,
We will break it down,
 Aunty, tira, lira, lo!

Allegretto.

1. Ah! mon beau châ-teau, Ma tant', ti-re, li-re, li-re; Ah! mon beau châ-teau, Ma tant', ti-re, li-re, lo.
3. Nous pai-'rons ran-çons, Ma tant', ti-re, li-re, li-re; Nous pai-'rons ran-çons, Ma tant', ti-re, li-re, lo?
5. De jo-lis bi-joux, Ma tant', ti-re, li-re, li-re; De jo-lis bi-joux, Ma tant', ti-re, li-re, lo.

But we'll ransom pay,
   Aunty, tira, lira, lira,
But we'll ransom pay,
   Aunty, tira, lira, lo!

What price will you pay?
   Aunty, tira, lira, lira,
What price will you pay?
   Aunty, tira, lira, lo!

We'll give pretty jewels,
   Aunty, tira, lira, lira,
We'll give pretty jewels,
   Aunty, tira, lira, lo!

No, we won't take jewels,
   Aunty, tira, lira, lira,
No, we won't take jewels,
   Aunty, tira, lira, lo!

We will give toy ships,
   Aunty, tira, lira, lira,
We will give toy ships,
   Aunty, tira, lira, lo!

No, we won't take ships,
   Aunty, tira, lira, lira,
No, we won't take ships,
   Aunty, tira, lira, lo!

We'll give ginger-men,
   Aunty, tira, lira, lira,
We'll give ginger-men,
   Aunty, tira, lira, lo!

We'll take ginger-men,
   Aunty, tira, lira, lira,
We'll take ginger-men,
   Aunty, tira, lira, lo!

2. Nous le dé - trui - rons, Ma tant', ti - re, li - re, li - re; Nous le dé - trui - rons, Ma tant', ti - re, li - re, lo.
4. Que nous donn-'rez-vous, Ma tant', ti - re, li - re, li - re; Que nous donn-'rez-vous, Ma tant', ti - re, li - re, lo?
6. Nous n'en vou-lons pas, Ma tant', ti - re, li - re, li - re; Nous n'en vou-lons pas, Ma tant', ti - re, li - re, lo!

The Style in the Bourbonnais

Love me, fair;
Curl your hair;
'Tis the style in the Bourbonnais —
Love me, fair;
Curl your hair;
Do you like the fashion there?

One and two,
I like you!
'Tis the style in the Bourbonnais —
One and two,
I like you!
Here we are two friends true!

The Bourbonnais is an old province in central France, where once the Dukes of Bourbon had their castle and stronghold.

Ho! Drummer Lad!

Ho! drummer lad,
Come home from war so far away;
There at your belt
A pretty, pretty rose so gay!
　　Rat-tat-a-tat!
　　Drums beat like that!
A pretty, pretty rose so gay!

King's daughter fair,
A-standing at her window said:
"Ho! drummer lad!
Will you give me your rosy red?"
        Rat-tat-a-tat!
        Drums beat like that—
"Will you give me your rosy red?"

Pray, King and Sire,
Your daughter,—may she be my bride?
Nay, drummer lad!
You're far too poor to suit my pride!
        Rat-tat-a-tat!
        Drums beat like that!
You're far too poor to suit my pride!

Ah! but, my King,
I've three ships on the ocean blue;
One bears my gold,
The other gems of every hue!
        Rat-tat-a-tat!
        Drums beat like that!
The other gems of every hue!

Best is the third;—
To bear my sweetheart home for me!
Ho! drummer lad!
Say, who can your father be?
        Rat-tat-a-tat!
        Drums beat like that!
Say, who can your father be?

Master and Sire,
My father's England's lord and King!
Take then the maid,
And wedding bells for you shall ring!
        Rat-tat-a-tat!
        Drums beat like that!
And wedding bells for you shall ring!

Nay! 'Tis too late!
Thanks, but she's not beyond compare!
In my own land
Are other pretty maids as fair!
     Rat-tat-a-tat!
     Drums beat like that!
Are other pretty maids as fair!

To Nantes, to Nantes

To Nantes, to Nantes there comes a fleet,
 (*Skip, fair one, and lift your feet*)
Behold three ships filled full of wheat.
  Skip, fair one, my pretty one,—
   Skip, fair one, and lift your feet!

Three ladies come those ships to greet,
 (*Skip, fair one, and lift your feet*)
Good sailor, how much is your wheat?
  Skip, fair one, my pretty one,—
   Skip, fair one, and lift your feet!

Full measure at six francs I'll mete,
(Skip, fair one, and lift your feet)
Pray come and see,—'tis good and sweet
Skip, fair one, my pretty one,—
Skip, fair one, and lift your feet!

She's on his ship, but O deceit!
(Skip, fair one, and lift your feet)
He starts to sail away, the cheat!
Skip, fair one, my pretty one,—
Skip, fair one, and lift your feet!

Oh, take me back, I do entreat!
(Skip, fair one, and lift your feet)
I hear my children cry and greit!
Skip, fair one, my pretty one,—
Skip, fair one, and lift your feet!

Nantes is a beautiful old city on the banks of the river Loire in Brittany. It stands so near the Atlantic Ocean that it is a great place for ships, for ship-building and fisheries.

Violet, You Grow Double, Double!

I've a long, long voyage for some one,
And I don't know who should go,
If I gave the lark my message,
He would let the whole world know!
Violet, you grow double, double,
Violet, double you will grow!

Nightingale, from fresh green forests,
On this errand will you go?
Nightingale his flight is winging
To the loved one's far chateau.
Violet, you grow double, double,
Violet, double you will grow!

There he finds the doors fast bolted,
By a window enters, lo!
Sees the ladies, all at table;
Now he greets the merry row.
Violet, you grow double, double,
Violet, double you will grow!

O, good day! Good day, my ladies!
And to ma'mselle there, heigho!
Master begs you'll not forget him,—
I am sent to tell you so!
  Violet, you grow double, double,
    Violet, double you will grow!

Ah, but I've forgotten others,
Why not him, I'd like to know?
He who'll not do his own errands
Should forgotten be, I trow!
  Violet, you grow double, double,
    Violet, double you will grow!

173

These ladies are wearing the costume in style in the days of Joan of Arc, the young girl who saved France from English invaders. (1412-1431).

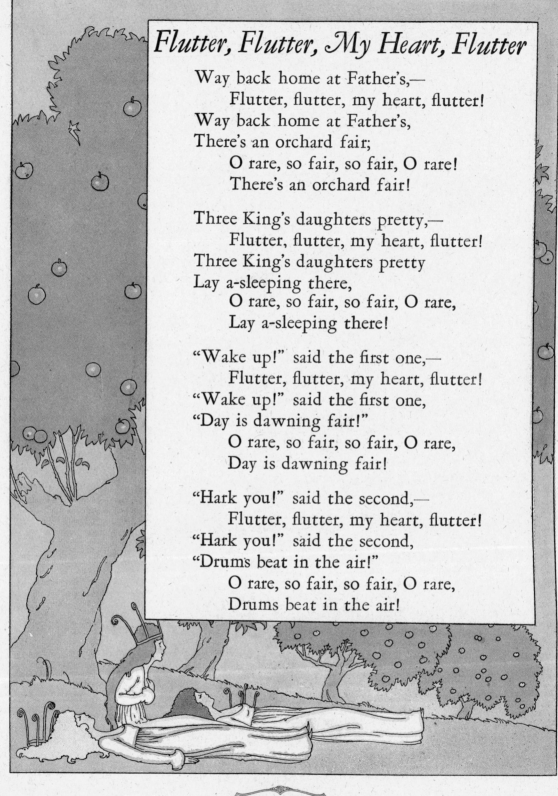

Flutter, Flutter, My Heart, Flutter

Way back home at Father's,—
    Flutter, flutter, my heart, flutter!
Way back home at Father's,
There's an orchard fair;
    O rare, so fair, so fair, O rare!
    There's an orchard fair!

Three King's daughters pretty,—
    Flutter, flutter, my heart, flutter!
Three King's daughters pretty
Lay a-sleeping there,
    O rare, so fair, so fair, O rare,
    Lay a-sleeping there!

"Wake up!" said the first one,—
    Flutter, flutter, my heart, flutter!
"Wake up!" said the first one,
"Day is dawning fair!"
    O rare, so fair, so fair, O rare,
    Day is dawning fair!

"Hark you!" said the second,—
    Flutter, flutter, my heart, flutter!
"Hark you!" said the second,
"Drums beat in the air!"
    O rare, so fair, so fair, O rare,
    Drums beat in the air!

"Truly," said the third one,—
　　Flutter, flutter, my heart, flutter!
"Truly," said the third one,
"'Tis my sweetheart there!"
　　O rare, so fair, so fair, O rare,
　　'Tis my sweetheart there!

Off he goes to battle,—
　　Flutter, flutter, my heart, flutter!
Off he goes to battle,
Bold to do and dare!
　　O rare, so fair, so fair, O rare,
　　Bold to do and dare!

If he wins the battle,—
　　Flutter, flutter, my heart, flutter!
If he wins the battle,
Him I'll love, I swear!
　　O rare, so fair, so fair, O rare!
　　Him I'll love, I swear!

Losing too, I'll love him,—
　　Flutter, flutter, my heart, flutter!
Always I will love him,
Whate'er betides, whate'er!
　　O rare, so fair, so fair, O rare!
　　Whate'er betides, whate'er!

The Tower! On Guard!

Two children take hands to represent the castle tower. The Captain and the Colonel, who are threatening to take the castle, walk around these two children, singing their part. The great Duke of Bourbon and his son are seated at a little distance, surrounded by their soldiers.

The Captain and the Colonel

The **tow**er—on guard, now! The tower—on guard, now,
Or we'll capture the castle!

The Castle

You can't, I tell you! You can't, I tell you!
You can't capture this castle!

LE CAPITAINE ET LE COLONEL.

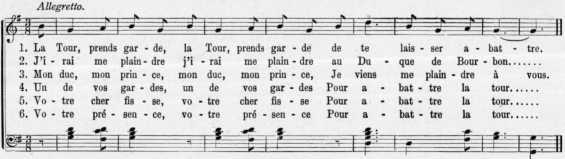

1. La Tour, prends gar - de, la Tour, prends gar - de de te lais - ser a - bat - tre.
2. J'i - rai me plain - dre j'i - rai me plain - dre au Du - que de Bour - bon.......
3. Mon duc, mon prin - ce, mon duc, mon prin - ce, Je viens me plain - dre à vous.
4. Un de vos gar - des, un de vos gar - des Pour a - bat - tre la tour......
5. Vo - tre cher fis - se, vo - tre cher fis - se Pour a - bat - tre la tour......
6. Vo - tre pré - sen - ce, vo - tre pré - sen - ce Pour a - bat - tre la tour......

The Captain and the Colonel

We'll go for help to the Duke of Bourbon;*
He will capture the castle!

The Castle

Then go and bring him; then go and bring him;
He can't capture this castle!

*(The Captain and the Colonel,
bending a knee before the Duke)*

Great Duke of Bourbon! Great Duke of Bourbon,
We come begging a favor.

LA TOUR.

Allegretto.

1. Nous n'a - vons gar - de nous n'a - vons gar - de de nous lais - ser a - bat - tre.
2. Va - t'en te plain - dre, Va - t'en te plain - dre au Du - que de Bour - bon......

Le duc:—

1. Mon cap - i - tain - e, mon co - lo - nel, Que me de - man - dez - vous?....
2. Al - lez, mon gar - de, al - lez, mon gar - de, Pour a - bat - tre la tour.....
3. Al - lez, mon fis - se, al - lez, mon fis - se, Pour a - bat - tre la tour.....
4. Je vais moi - mê - me, je vais moi - mê - me, Pour a - bat - tre la tour.....

Nursery Friends
from France

The Duke

Speak out, my Captain; speak out, my Colonel,—
  What boon is it you're asking?

The Captain and the Colonel

We ask a soldier; we ask a soldier;
  To help capture the castle.

The Duke

Then go, my soldier! Then go, my soldier,
And help capture the castle!

The soldier goes with the officers and all three march around the castle singing:

The tower—on guard, now! The tower—on guard, now,
Or we'll capture the castle.

The Castle

You can't, I tell you! You can't I, tell you!
You can't capture this castle.

The officers return to the Duke demanding two, then three, then four more soldiers, each time circling about the castle and singing their song of challenge, to be scoffed at by the tower. When all the soldiers are gone, the followers of the Captain and the Colonel bow before the Duke and sing:

Pray send your son, now! Pray send your son, now,
To help capture the castle.

The same play is again carried on around the castle. The troop then returns to the Duke and says:

Pray come, your highness! Pray come, your highness,
To help capture the castle.

The Duke

I come myself, then! I come myself, then!
And I'll capture the castle.

The Duke puts himself at the head of the troop and tries to force apart the hands of the children who represent the castle. If he fails, each of the children who follow him, tries in turn. The one who succeeds becomes Duke.

*There were many famous Dukes of Bourbon. They had a castle and stronghold in the Bourbonnais, a province of central France. One of the most famous of these dukes was Charles (1490-1527) who was made Constable of France, and called Constable Bourbon. Constable Bourbon was an able general, but he had a grudge against the French King, Francis I, and caused him a great deal of trouble in his time. From this great family of the Bourbons came Henry IV of France. It also furnished a line of kings to Spain and to Naples.

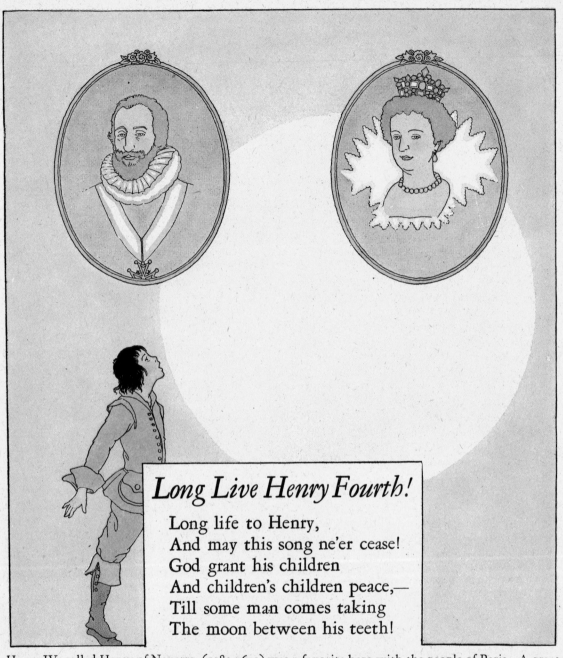

Long Live Henry Fourth!

Long life to Henry,
And may this song ne'er cease!
God grant his children
And children's children peace,—
Till some man comes taking
The moon between his teeth!

Henry IV, called Henry of Navarre, (1589-1610) was a favorite hero with the people of Paris. A great statue of him on horseback stands on the Pont Neuf, one of the principal bridges of Paris.

Henry IV was the first King of France from the family of the Bourbons and was related no doubt to that famous Duke, who is always being summoned by the children of France to take the tower, when they play "The tower, on guard!" Henry's children's children did indeed keep their seats on the throne of France for two hundred years,—not till someone came "taking the moon between his teeth!" but until the French Revolution swept his great, great, great, great, great grandson, Louis XVI, off the throne, and made a republic with a president at its head, instead of a King. To this very day, however, Henry's children's children are still claiming the throne of France.

If the King Should Give to Me

If the King should give to me
His grand city of Paree,
And should say that I must leave
My sweetheart behind, you see,
I would say to King Henree:
"Pray you take back your Paree,—
I prefer my sweetheart fair;
My sweetheart means more to me!'

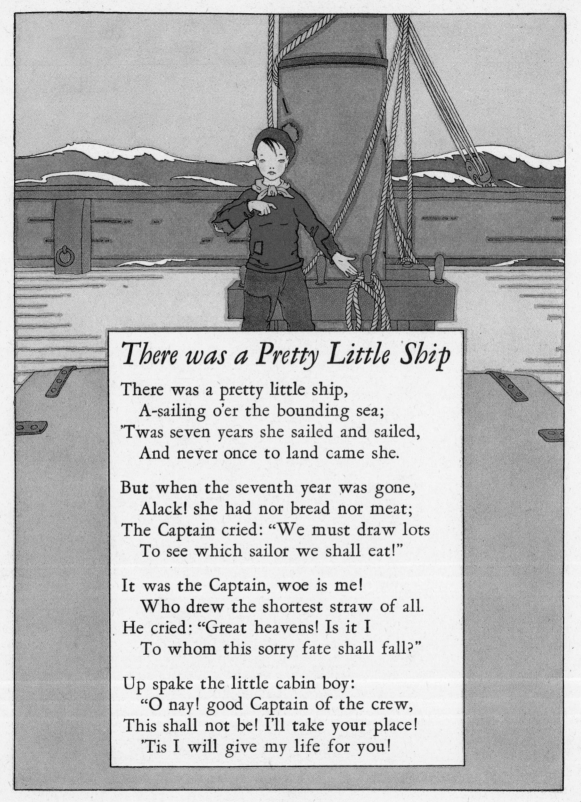

There was a Pretty Little Ship

There was a pretty little ship,
    A-sailing o'er the bounding sea;
'Twas seven years she sailed and sailed,
    And never once to land came she.

But when the seventh year was gone,
    Alack! she had nor bread nor meat;
The Captain cried: "We must draw lots
    To see which sailor we shall eat!"

It was the Captain, woe is me!
    Who drew the shortest straw of all.
He cried: "Great heavens! Is it I
    To whom this sorry fate shall fall?"

Up spake the little cabin boy:
    "O nay! good Captain of the crew,
This shall not be! I'll take your place!
    'Tis I will give my life for you!"

"But first I beg you let me climb
    High up atop the mast," he cried.
He climbs atop the tall main mast,
    And looks about on every side.

He strains his eyes for sight of land;
    And now, ah! now, he sings from there:
"I see the towers of Babylon,
    And Barbary's green shore so fair!

I see the white sheep on the plain,
    A shepherdess beneath a tree!
I see our Captain's daughter, too,
    And lo! she feeds her pigeons three!"

O sing! You're safe! brave cabin boy!
    On yonder land is food to eat!
The Captain's daughter is your bride;
    And yours the ship beneath your feet!

*Nursery Friends
from France*

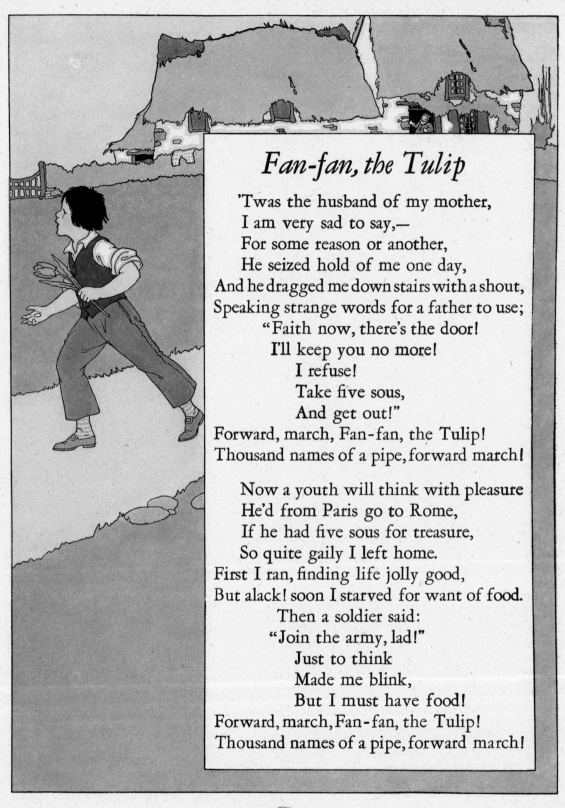

Fan-fan, the Tulip

'Twas the husband of my mother,
I am very sad to say,—
For some reason or another,
He seized hold of me one day,
And he dragged me down stairs with a shout,
Speaking strange words for a father to use;
"Faith now, there's the door!
I'll keep you no more!
I refuse!
Take five sous,
And get out!"
Forward, march, Fan-fan, the Tulip!
Thousand names of a pipe, forward march!

Now a youth will think with pleasure
He'd from Paris go to Rome,
If he had five sous for treasure,
So quite gaily I left home.
First I ran, finding life jolly good,
But alack! soon I starved for want of food.
Then a soldier said:
"Join the army, lad!"
Just to think
Made me blink,
But I must have food!
Forward, march, Fan-fan, the Tulip!
Thousand names of a pipe, forward march!

Hearing cannon roar and rattle,
I was filled with sudden fears,
Till I saw march into battle
All our fine old grenadiers.
For an instant they stood on parade,
Then, egad! to myself I said that day:
"Come, come, my bold boy,
Fan-fan, you're no toy!
Quick away!
They sha'n't say
You're afraid!"
Forward, march, Fan-fan, the **Tulip!**
Thousand names of a pipe, forward march!

Twenty years I was a soldier,
Ever up at duty's call,
But when battles once were over,
I'd no enemies at all.
Prayers of poor conquered men, sad to hear,
Made me ever fly to help them anew.
What I did perhaps
For unhappy chaps,
They might do,
In turn, true,
For my mother dear.
Forward, march, Fan-fan, the Tulip!
Thousand names of a pipe, forward march!

Then the time came when my father
Asked for help when poor and ill.
What a moment to get even
If I'd kept my anger still!
Ah, but true soldier boys every one,
Always helpful to their parents you'll find,—
Father did not care
If I starved, but there!—
Never mind!
That's behind!
I am his son.
Forward, march, Fan-fan, the Tulip!
Thousand names of a pipe, forward march!

Hark! Don't You Hear, Rub Dub! the Drum

Hark! don't you hear, rub dub! the drum?
 Quick, come and dance now!
Hark! don't you hear, rub dub! the drum?
It calls you villagers — "Come, come!"

 Fie on the city!
 Life there's slow,—the pity!
No one is gay with lively dance, my boys!
But the village,—ah, there men are witty;
In the village good folk laugh at noise!

Hark! don't you hear, rub dub! the drum?
 Quick, come and dance now!
Hark! don't you hear, rub dub! the drum?
It calls you villagers,—"Come, come!"

 How now, Lisette,
 You're not ready yet!
What keeps you back? The combing of your hair?
Bagpipe's calling, little gay coquette;
And young Colin awaits you there!

Hark! don't you hear, rub dub! the drum?
 Quick, come and dance now!
Hark! don't you hear, rub dub, the drum?
It calls you villagers,—"Come, come!"

CONTENTS

THE MAP OF

France

BELLE ISL

N

W ← → E

S